FUNNY & FUNNIER

Shirshendu Mukhopadhyay started his career as a school teacher and is now on the staff of the *Ananda Bazar Patrika* in Kolkata. He is associated with the Bengali magazine, *Desh*. His first novel *Ghunpoka* was published in the annual Puja edition of *Desh*. His first children's novel was called *Manojder Adbhut Baari*. He has received the Vidyasagar Award in 1985 for his contribution to children's literature. He has also received the Ananda Purashkar twice and the Sahitya Akademi award for one of his novels.

*

Palash Baran Pal is a physicist who works at the Saha Institute of Nuclear Physics, Kolkata. His previous translations from the Bengali include stories by Rabindranath Tagore and Parashuram. His translations into Bengali include collections of poems by Pablo Neruda, Jacques Prevert and Matsuo Basho. Apart from translation works, he has also published a collection of folktales, a treatise on linguistics, several books of popular science, and, of course, many research papers in Physics.

*

Abhijit Gupta teaches English at Jadavpur University. He is a co-editor of the *Book History in India* series of which two volumes have been published and is also the associate editor for South Asia for the *Oxford Companion to the Book*. His other research areas include science fiction, graphic novels, crime fiction and the 19th century.

Funny & Funnier

Stories *by*
Shirshendu Mukhopadhyay

Translated by
Palash Baran Pal & Abhijit Gupta

Illustrations by
Uma Krishnaswamy

SCHOLASTIC
New York Toronto London Auckland
Sydney New Delhi Hong Kong

Published by Scholastic India Pvt. Ltd.
A subsidiary of Scholastic Inc., New York, 10012 (USA).
Publishers since 1920, with international operations in Canada,
Australia, New Zealand, the United Kingdom, Mexico, India,
Argentina, and Hong Kong.

For information regarding permission, write to:
Scholastic India Pvt. Ltd.
Golf View Corporate Tower-A, 3rd Floor,
DLF Phase-V, Gurgaon-122002 (India)

Typeset in 12.5/17 AGaramond by SÜRYA, New Delhi

First edition: June 2010
Reprint: July, August, September 2010; March, October 2011;
January 2012; February , October 2014; January, March 2016; September 2(

ISBN-13: 978-81-8477-465-8

Printed at J J Offset Printers, Noida

Contents

Translators' Note

The stories appeared in various periodicals over a few decades. The earliest one is probably 'The Smell Is Very Suspicious', which came out in the 1970s. Rather than digging out the original versions, we have followed the text of the collection '*Goyenda Barada Charan Samagra O Anyanya*' (Nath Publishing, 2007) for our translation.

Palash Baran Pal
Abhijit Gupta

Acknowledgements

Palash Baran Pal wants to thank Shoili Pal and Proyag Pal for carefully reading earlier versions of his translations and suggesting improvements.

No Joy for the King

There was no longer any joy in the life of the king. A great deal of labour had gone into cheering him up. Songs had been sung, dances arranged, the court jester had performed a thousand antics; plays, farces, fairs, carnivals, prayers, rituals—everything had been tried out. From the eastern provinces came pineapples, apples came from the snow-bound north; the west sent apricots, grapes and pistachios while sweets made of sweetened cream and cottage cheese came from all over. Chinese and European cooks served up delicious meals all through the day. The king saw, heard, and tasted everything, but every hour on the hour, thunderous sighs shook his chest, 'It's no good, I don't feel well at all.'

All day long the royal physician sat with closed eyes, with his finger on the king's pulse. The pulse raced, skipped, plodded or stumbled as it saw fit. The physician muttered to himself and prepared decoctions from roots, herbs and leaves, and gave them to the king. The king took his physic dutifully. Then came the sigh, 'It's no good, I don't feel well at all.'

In order to cheer the king, his princes and generals annexed nearly a dozen neighbouring states and brought their defeated kings captive. The king looked at them. Then he sighed, without realising he had done so, 'Nothing feels good any more.'

The prime minister then arranged for the king to go on a pilgrimage and visit sights. The king travelled to over a hundred holy places and distant lands, with a large retinue in tow. Then he returned, washed his hands and face, sat on the throne, and announced, 'Alas, alas, I don't feel well at all.'

The jester, worn out from non-stop japery, gave

up his post. The royal dancer was afflicted with gout. The court singer lost his voice. The musicians suffered from aching wrists and fingers. The chefs wanted to go on leave. The court physician entered a state of senility. The general took early retirement. The prime minister's wife began to suspect he was losing his mind. The royal priest had burnt so much sacrificial ghee that the slightest whiff of it now made him pass out. The king's subjects were showing signs of unrest. The scholars at court were engaged day and night in researching the king's melancholy. The royal astrologer filled reams of papers with calculations of the king's horoscope.

One evening, the king sat with a morose look on his face, in his vast palace garden. Thousands of flowers bloomed in a riot of colours and scents. Bees buzzed, birds cooed in honeyed tones. There were swans on the ornamental pool, and its waters rippled in the soft breeze.

For a while, the king sat silent. Then he suddenly let out a roar like a lion, 'Off with his head!'

Next to the king, the prime minister was muttering to himself, a sure sign of madness. He jumped at the king's outburst, 'Whose head, your majesty?'

Somewhat abashed, the king said, 'Actually, I haven't thought about that yet. I suddenly felt it would be a good idea to have someone beheaded.'

The prime minister said, 'Think, your majesty, think hard. Say the word, and we will bring the head in no time.'

It had been a long time since the king had asked for anything. The prime minister now began to entertain hopes that a suitable head might cheer up the king. Heads were very easily available in the kingdom.

The next morning, after the business of the court was done, the king called the prime minister over and said, 'Come to think of it, it was not a head that I wanted. It was something else, but for the life of me I cannot remember what.'

That evening, the king was taking a walk on the vast palace terrace, followed by the royal dog, the hookah and paan bearers and the prime minister. As he walked, his gaze fell on the village across the river, and he shouted, 'Burn the crone's cottage down! Set the crone's cottage on fire!'

The prime minister stopped muttering. He stood with folded hands in front of the king and said, 'As you please, sire. Just say the crone's name.'

The king stared in astonishment, 'What did I say just now?'

'Didn't you ask us to burn down the crone's cottage?'

The king scratched his neck and said, 'Did I? Let me think about it.'

That night the king was heard shouting in his sleep, 'Nettles! Whip with stinging nettles!'

The next morning, it was all over the palace: the king had asked for stinging nettles. Everyone looked terrified.

The prime minister whispered in the king's ear, 'Your majesty. Just tell us who it is you want whipped with the nettles. Nettles are being obtained from the western mountains even as we speak.'

'Nettles?' the king looked on in amazement and became lost in thought.

The sun set on the western mountains. Cartloads of stinging nettles waited in the palace courtyard. But the king's mind was not on nettles.

The king sat in the gaming-room and played chess with his companions. His face was grave, and he looked distracted. The worried companions were trying to make the king win by deliberately playing weak moves. But the king was making even weaker moves.

As he played, the king pulled once on the pipe of his hookah and observed, 'Should we bury them alive?'

The prime minister was close by. He stopped muttering and looked up, gratified. 'Very good idea, your majesty. Just say the word and it is done.'

The king stared as if he had gone mad. 'What is a very good idea? Nothing is good anywhere. I don't feel good at all.'

The prime minister lapsed into his usual depression and resumed muttering.

The next morning, the king went hunting, with a large contingent of men, weapons, horses and chariots. Animals such as deer, rabbits and birds had been tethered at various points in the forest so that the king could hunt easily. There was a tiger as well. The king spent a long time riding about on horseback but did not fire a single arrow. At noon, as the king lunched on pilau and meat curry, he shouted, 'Help, help! Too many ghosts!'

The prime minister rose immediately, wiping his curry-stained hand on his head. He stood in front of the king and said, 'Just say the word, your majesty. Ghosts, eh? Nothing to worry about at all, sire. We will send for the exorcist, and all the ghosts in the kingdom will be impaled forthwith.'

The king gaped. 'Not ghosts, not exactly ghosts. Did I say ghosts? But tell me this, do ghosts have migraine?'

The prime minister saw a ray of hope in this, and said expectantly, 'Well, there are physicians for ghosts in the case of migraine. They know what the cure is.'

The king became grave. 'No, I was not thinking about ghosts. I don't feel good any more.'

A few days later, on a moonlit night, the king sat next to the queen in a balcony in the women's quarters. Suddenly he said, 'Come O queen, let us eat wet rice in the moonlight.'

At first the queen was surprised. Then she quickly called for the prime minister.

The prime minister stood with folded hands and said, 'That is very easily done, sire.' Then he called out, 'Men, get some wet rice, on the double.'

The king stared in astonishment. 'Wet rice? What on earth is wet rice?'

'Rice in water, your majesty, usually eaten by poor people. But you yourself asked for wet rice.'

'I did? Well then, I must have. Don't know what I say nowadays. Nothing feels right any more.'

The prime minister went back. But that night,

he summoned the four most subtle spies in the kingdom and said to them, 'You will each take turns and keep a constant watch on his majesty. I want him watched twenty-four hours.'

The next morning one of the spies reported, 'At dawn, the king got out of his bed and crawled about on the floor for a long time.'

Another one said, 'The king keeps whimpering and asking for a red dress.'

The third spy said, 'The king just snatched a pastry from a maid's little boy and ate it himself.'

The fourth one said, 'I have nothing much to report. I only heard the king burping at regular intervals, and saying, "What now? All is done, what now?"'

The following morning, the first spy reported, 'I have been spotted by his majesty. Last night, when I peeped through the window, I saw his majesty looking straight at me. He said, "Keeping watch, eh?" and promptly fell asleep.'

The second spy said, 'Y'r honour, I was actually under the bed. At midnight, the king crawled under the bed and said to me, "Come out, you'll get centipedes in your ear."'

The third spy scratched his ear and said shyly, 'I was pretending to be a gardener and was trimming hedges in the garden. The king called me in a very loving voice and said, "A good spy has to be good at everything. Is that any way to trim hedges? Let me show you how it is done." Then he took the shears from me and trimmed the hedges.'

But the fourth and the most expert spy Rakhohari was nowhere to be found. The prime minister began to get worried.

In the meantime, Rakhohari was not going in for any fancy stuff. He had been standing outside the king's bedroom in the morning. As soon as the king came out, he touched his feet and said, 'Your majesty, I am the spy Rakhohari. I have been asked to keep a watch on you.'

Though surprised, the king smiled graciously. He yawned and said, 'Good, good, carry on with your work.'

After this, Rakhohari began to follow the king like a hawk.

Nothing much happened till the afternoon. The king had just popped a paan into his mouth after lunch. Suddenly he burst out, 'Pinch hard! Pinch very hard.'

Instantly, the spy Rakhohari applied a humungous pinch to the king's stomach. The king made a strangled noise and said, 'Go easy go easy! That hurt.'

Rakhohari said, 'But you asked for it.'

The king patted himself on his stomach, but he smiled.

Evening followed afternoon. The king went for a walk in the palace gardens. Suddenly he shouted, 'Stick out a leg.' Immediately, Rakhohari brought the king down with a tackle. Lying on the ground, the king blinked several times. Rakhohari pulled the king up, dusted him down and touched his feet. The king breathed heavily and went 'Hmm.'

The king did nothing out of the ordinary till night. Rakhohari followed him into the bedroom, and hid beside a cupboard in full view of the king. The king looked sidelong at him, and smiled briefly. But he did not say anything. However, shortly after going to bed, he suddenly started demanding in a high-pitched voice, 'Want a cold bath, want a cold ba . . .' In a flash, Rakhohari picked up a golden pitcher filled with rose and kewra water and upended it on the king's head.

The king started, sneezed, coughed and sat up. But he did not look very displeased. He looked at Rakhohari and smiled, 'Fine. Now go sleep.'

Rakhohari did not sleep however. He stayed on guard.

The king awoke the next morning and yawned. Then he suddenly said, 'Quick, a dagger to the heart . . .' Immediately, Rakhohari took out his dagger and pointed it at the king's chest.

The flabbergasted king said, 'Alright alright, that's enough. I had completely forgotten about you.'

As Rakhohari put away his dagger, the king

began to roar with laughter. He laughed so much that everyone in the palace came running. He clutched his sides in mirth and said, 'Oh, this is such fun. I am feeling so happy, so happy.'

The prime minister also arrived on the scene. He patted the king on his back. 'Such a relief, your majesty. All is well again.'

The king choked as he carried on laughing. 'Ho ho ho. This is such fun, such fun.'

From that point, the king was completely cured of his gloom. But then, a new problem arose. The king chuckled all the time without any rhyme or reason, even when bad news was given to him. Loss in battle? Tee-hee. Someone dead? Tee-hee. Famine in the kingdom? Tee-hee. Rebellion in the south? Tee-hee.

Now the prime minister has to think twice as hard to stop the king from laughing.

Translated by Abhijit Gupta

Bidhu Daroga

There was great excitement that year when Bidhu daroga was transferred to our locality. This was in the time of British rule when even the sight of a policeman would send blameless and law-abiding citizens scurrying for cover. On one occasion, some minor Swadeshi leader had come to deliver a speech under the banyan tree. A crowd of about five hundred had gathered, and were in a state of high excitement after being harangued by the speaker. At that moment, an extremely emaciated-looking policeman in a red turban happened to pass by, on his way home after buying spinach. The five hundred-strong crowd just turned tail and ran for their lives. The Swadeshi leader sat under the tree, lit a dejected bidi and sighed, 'Hopeless.' On another occasion, a boatload of people was about to make the evening crossing when the daroga and some other policemen boarded the ferry. Immediately, for no obvious reason, almost all the passengers jumped out of the boat and waded to the shore through knee-deep water. The pandit of the village primary school also happened to be among them. When we quizzed him later about the incident, he said sheepishly, 'Well, I ran away since everyone else was running away as well. Nothing is as infectious as fear.'

This will give you some idea about how formidable the police was in those days. But Bidhu daroga was made of even sterner stuff. Such was his reputation that he once caused a cow and a tiger to drink from the same ghat, as the saying goes. The first thing he did after taking up his posting was to issue a proclamation that on the following market day, a cow and a tiger would drink from the pond to the north of the constabulary. All members of the public were urged to witness this event for themselves.

A huge crowd gathered by the pond on market day. The massive form of Bidhu daroga could be seen on the steps of the ghat, occupying his chair of office. No one had ever seen him laugh or smile. His gaze was so fierce that those on whom it fell would quail and quickly change their position, so much so that my uncle, the body-builder, was forced to shift his position thrice till he stood among the rushes. No one dared speak out aloud, but whispered and mumbled among themselves. All had heard the proverb about the cow and the tiger drinking from the same ghat but no one had actually seen such a spectacle. A cow with twisted horns stood tethered by the water; she belonged to Haru Mondal and was known to have quite a temper. Of the tiger there was no sight yet, and the crowd waited with bated breath.

It was not a long wait. The Prabartak Circus had been playing in the next village since the last new moon and a team of bullocks arrived from there pulling a circus cart. On the cart was a cage, and inside the cage was a drowsy-looking tiger, causing some to speculate that the beast was doped with opium.

Whatever be the case, the ring-master of the circus—a thin man clad in black singlet and tights—stood with his whip near the gate of the cage. Two more men unlatched the door and raised it. A small stampede ensued, and the crowd put some distance between itself and the cage. Only the ring-master, Haru Mondal, Bidhu daroga and the two men from the circus remained on the ghat steps. The police constables also stood some distance away—a tiger out of its cage was no joke.

The tiger gave every sign of being an opium-eater. The ring-master cracked his whip repeatedly, and then poked and prodded, but he simply refused to leave the cage. Three times he yawned, making a sound usually made by very old men. The daroga was furious, 'Drag the poltroon out of the cage!' The ring-master saluted, 'He must have taken fright at you, sir.'

After much effort, the tiger was dragged out of the cage by its leash. But even then he showed no sign of activity. He stretched and preened exactly like a cat, and then began to look all around. There seemed something wrong with his sight, for he would keep peering at the near distance. Bidhu daroga roared, 'Take them both to the water.'

Both Haru Mondal and the ring-master began to pull the leashes of their respective charges. After much pulling and dragging, both of them stood side by side near the water, but none of them could be induced to drink. Now this could not be allowed to happen—after all, the daroga babu's prestige was at stake. Haru Mondal caressed his cow's dewlap and spoke words of endearment, 'Bhagabati, child, drink the water. Just this once, child, and I will never ask you again. Don't mind that goat-faced kitten: he has rheumy eyes and rotten teeth, he is nothing but a scaredy cat.'

The ring-master too was not idle. He cracked his whip and twisted the tiger's tail, '*Drink water, Bengal tiger*,' he roared, '*Drink, come come, have courage. The cow will fly and show her tail. Drink drink . . .'*

The daroga roared again: 'Untie them both. Let them drink together.'

This was speedily done. Haru Mondal released his cow and whispered in her ear, 'I kept you thirsty, did not give you water for one whole day, all for daroga babu's sake. Now drink, drink the whole pond dry.'

The ring-master did likewise, and added, *'You had no water for two days, Bengal tiger, now drink.'*

And drink they did. It was a sight no one had ever seen before. A tiger and a cow standing side by side like obedient children and drinking from the same ghat. A huge cheer went up for the daroga. The local apothecary, Dukari Haldar, broke into an impromptu song: 'All praise Bidhu, O praised be th-o-o-o-u! / At whose bidding drink the tiger and the co-o-o-w . . .'

But the cheers had hardly faded away, and Dukari Haldar had not yet finished expelling breath upon the co-o-o-w, when the tiger raised his head from the water and looked at the cow. The cow too looked at the tiger. Both of them breathed heavily. The tiger was familiar with the smell of cows, and started sniffing at the cow, probably because he could not see very well and was not sure what was standing next to him. The cow had never seen a tiger before but this did not seem to bother her one bit. In fact, she glared angrily at the tiger. She was a rascally animal who regularly uprooted her stake, and there was hardly any villager who had not been tossed by her. The tiger's strange behaviour must have annoyed her, for she suddenly advanced upon him, and huffed full upon his face.

Bidhu daroga tweaked his moustache in pleasure at the sight. True, he did not smile, but there was a hint of laughter in his eyes, and in the quivering of his cheek and jowl. After all, it was not every day that a tiger and cow drank from the same ghat.

The tiger retreated a couple of steps. He had long got out of the habit of getting into a fight.

But the cow was really ill-tempered, and was spoiling for a fight. She tossed her horns menacingly and advanced another couple of steps. The tiger continued to back away. Suddenly, the cow let out a stentorian moo. Lowering her head, she broke into a lumbering run and head-butted the tiger. The tiger had forgotten how to fight. Completely taken aback at being butted, he shook himself out of his stupor and leapt out of reach, to the top of the ghat steps. From below, up came the cow.

Bidhu daroga rose from his chair and nimbly got out of the way. Those present were open-mouthed with surprise. Had anyone ever seen such a sight? What a reversal of the laws of nature! The tiger was running for his life along the field next to the pond, while Haru's cow followed in hot pursuit, hell-bent upon butting the tiger. The tiger was yowling piteously while the cow bellowed majestically in reply. What a chase it was! Both tiger and cow kept on running, till the tiger began to struggle and show signs of exhaustion. All the while Haru Mondal had been shouting and yelling at his cow to turn back, but to no avail. The cow just kept going. The ringmaster burst into tears and blubbered, 'Harubhai, your crazy cow will kill my poor kitty.'

This could very well have happened. The tiger was on the verge of collapse and the rampaging cow was about to catch him when Haru Mondal lay down directly in his Bhagabati's path, and pleaded with her, 'We marvel at your deeds, O mother. I will bring you many more tigers and lions to play with, and you can butt them all to your heart's content. But now it's time for your fodder.'

On hearing these words, Bhagabati came to a halt and huffed noisily. Spying his chance, the tiger sprang back into the cage and tried to close the door by standing on his hind legs. The two men from the circus who were hovering nearby quickly lowered the grill gate. Overcome with relief, the tiger sat in one corner and panted noisily.

After this incident, Bidhu daroga's fame spread

like wildfire. Not only did cow and tiger drink together under his command, but the cow actually chased the tiger within an inch of his life. Such a man was not to be trifled with.

Suddenly everyone was on their best behaviour. Thieves and dacoits lay low, and even brawls became scarce. Older people would take off their shoes when they passed the constabulary and fold their hands in obeisance, as though it was a temple. And Bidhu daroga would smile—well, not exactly *smile*, but a smile would dangle from the ends of his moustache, from the tip of his nose, and from his eyebrows. Then everyone knew that Bidhu daroga was smiling, but not *smiling*, oh no. The local confectioner even invented new sweets with names such as 'Bidhu-Barfi' and 'Daroga's Delight'.

Bhagabati, too, had become quite famous. People flocked to see her not just from distant towns and villages, but from the cities as well. There were huge crowds every day. All came bearing mountains of food for Bhagabati—not just the usual gourds and pumpkins, but sandesh and rosogolla, as well as butter and ghee. Haru Mondal's cowshed was piled to the rafters with victuals. The local zamindar had gifted a nylon mosquito net to the miracle cow, and a matching set of satin pillows and cushions. All day long Bhagabati would chomp her way through the daily offerings; at night she sat against a pillow under the net, chewing cud contentedly until she drifted off to sleep. Not surprisingly, she had put on considerable weight. Sometimes, when she felt a bit overcome by the heat, her devotees would fan her vigorously with hand-fans till she was soothed. In Sahaganj, the Bhagabati High School came up in her name, while a new embrocation called 'Bhagabati Oil' also hit the market.

For some time, there was no topic of interest other than Bidhu daroga and Bhagabati. The proprietor of the circus rolled up his top and left. Since there were no other large animals in the vicinity, Bhagabati was not able to butt anyone. Her jaws ached with constant chewing.

Bidhu daroga was in a similar situation. The crime rate had fallen so drastically that he was getting no exercise at all. The local people brought him such quantities of chicken, eggs, mutton, vegetables and fish that he lost his appetite completely. He did not feel hungry any more. The very sight of food would set him yawning. Even his horse began to accumulate fat around its hocks. Every evening, the daroga would saddle his horse and dutifully go on his rounds, but there was absolutely nothing happening anywhere. A disgusted daroga would return to the constabulary and grimly smoke a hookah on the porch.

One morning a man turned up with a *rui* fish weighing half a maund, and sat worshipfully at the daroga's feet with folded hands. The sight of the enormous fish only caused the daroga to avert his face in distaste. The man, thinking that maybe the size of the fish had not been to the daroga's liking, said fearfully, 'Y'r honour, I don't have anything bigger than this in my pond. I am a small man, and my *rui* is not much bigger than a *punti*, but I had thought that y'r honour might enjoy . . .'

Bidhu daroga sighed mightily, and said, 'It is not that. It's just that I don't feel hungry any more. I have no appetite at all.'

The man touched his feet again and said, 'If I may be so bold, even the gods who have tasted divine nectar have no reason to feel hungry ever again, but don't we still offer them our choicest morsels? And do they not partake, even if they have no appetite? I am an old man, but I have never heard it said the high and mighty of the land ever feel hungry. They are like the gods, who do not ever crave food. But still they force themselves to eat, only for our sake. Y'r honour, only yokels and ne'er-do-wells like us are always hungry.'

The daroga was flattered at being referred to as both high and mighty. He smiled. Well, not exactly *smiled*, but his bald pate shone for a moment, a ripple passed through his jowls, and his stomach shook a few times, so that it seemed as if he was laughing. Then he sighed heavily and said, 'How is one supposed to get an appetite without exercise? There is nothing to do here, except sit in one place and turn to stone. And the folks here are pathetic—here is their daroga suffering from loss of appetite, and they can't even get up a decent theft or robbery. At least I could have gotten some exercise if there were crooks to chase. But you people have no feelings at all!'

The man beamed from ear to ear and once again touched the daroga's feet. 'That's exactly why I came, y'r honour. For the past few days, a kapalik—a practitioner of black magic—has set up under the banyan tree in the woods next to the burning ghat. He is a terrible man, y'r honour, and rides a tiger, and everyone's saying that he will make a human sacrifice tonight. There is great fear among the people, y'r honour.'

Bidhu daroga let out a terrific roar. Houses shook in their foundations, and the daroga's horse neighed in fear. Those who were nearby quickly sought shelter, children bawled, cats fled from the scene, dogs whimpered and the crows set up a terrible ruckus, thinking someone had fired a gun. The man who had brought the fish passed out for a few moments. When he came to, he rubbed his eyes and then beamed with pleasure. *This* was how a daroga was meant to be. He bowed and touched his feet once more.

It was pitch dark in the night when the daroga set off on horseback, towards the burning ghat in Safarganj. With him went a large party of constables, and other villagers. They made such a racket that the jackals fled and birds woke up chirping from their sleep. Small animals such as skunks, rabbits, weasels, mice and mongoose hid in their holes and shook in fear. The daroga reached the ancient banyan tree and roared, 'Where is the *kapalik*?'

There was no reply. The daroga switched on his five-battery torch and surveyed the scene. The reports were not untrue. There was a heap of dying embers, and the pug-marks of a tiger all around. A shiny cleaver lay next to a chopping block. The daroga whipped out his pistol and shouted again, 'Come out, you wretched creature!'

Everyone looked around in vain. Had he run away?

Suddenly a plaintive voice issued from the top of the tree. Someone called out, 'Y'r honour, here I am. Would you please hold the light, good sir? I am too far up the tree and can't get down by myself.'

Surprised, the daroga directed his torch upwards. The bearded kapalik and his red robes could be glimpsed through the branches and foliage, high up on the tree. 'Get down here,' said the daroga sternly. The kapalik came down slowly. He was a scrawny looking fellow and blinked fearfully in the glare of the torchlight. Then he suddenly fell at the feet of the daroga's horse and babbled, 'Begging your pardon, sir, begging your pardon.' The daroga, dismayed by the man's appearance and demeanour, demanded, 'Where is your tiger?'

'Sir, he clambered up a mango tree when he saw you coming. He is not very brave, sir.'

The daroga fixed him with a piercing glare and said, 'And where is the man to be sacrificed?'

The kapalik burst into tears. 'What sacrifice, y'r honour? I have begged, and threatened, and pleaded, but no one wants to be sacrificed. I can't blame them, for who would want to be sacrificed of their own will? But no one respects a kapalik if there isn't talk of a sacrifice or two; that's why I had spread the rumour. But I am no kapalik, y'r honour, can you not recognise me? I am the ring-master of Prabartak Circus.'

The ring-master! Everyone gaped in surprise. But so it was, if one looked closely at the kapalik's face through all the facial hair. Trembling with fear, the ring-master said, 'My tiger got a very bad name after being chased all over the countryside by Haru Mondal's thuggish cow. We were both thrown out of the circus. Since then, we have hardly had two square meals. All that talk about sacrifices is rubbish, we are both very timid creatures, y'r honour.'

The daroga smiled. Well, not exactly *smiled*,

but his eyebrows lifted, and his earlobes seemed to quiver, and the tips of his moustache turned up on their own. Everyone saw in the light of the torch—he did not smile, but still seemed to smile.

The ring-master and his tiger were placed under arrest and brought to the constabulary. Huge crowds gathered from all over. The ring-master received a haircut and a shave. The tiger was tied securely to a *kadam* tree where he hid his face in his paws and hung his head in shame.

Haru Mondol touched the daroga's feet and said, 'I have a petition, y'r honour. My Bhagabati has no appetite. She has nobody to play with and does not get any exercise. She does not want to eat anything. All the cows and bulls are scared of her, so they don't come near. So I was wondering if I could have the tiger. My Bhagabati would play with him, and have someone to butt. Her appetite will then return. I am ready to pay a hundred rupees for him.'

And so it happened. Haru Mondal dragged the tiger home on a leash, all the while telling people,

'Got him cheap, got a tiger cheap.'

But Bhagabati had become very lazy ever since she had begun to put on weight. She did not charge the tiger, but just sat there and huffed. The tiger was about to run away at this, but Haru Mondal whacked him with his sandals and dragged him back. He then tethered him next to Bhagabati.

Since then, the tiger has been staying in the cowshed, eating fish-bones or rice and scraps of meat. Sometimes he would try to feed from Bhagabati's fodder bowl, and then avert his face in distaste. Still, he would try. Sometimes, Bhagabati would lovingly lick him all over. The tiger would scratch her back with his paws.

People came from far and near to see them. After all, it was not every day that a tiger and a cow shared the same cowshed. Dukari the minstrel went about singing:

All sing praise in Bidhu's name
he's the light of our lives, our pride and fame.
Praise be Bhagabati, by whose side

in captivity, a tiger abides.
Once more to Bidhu give high praise
he turns days into nights, and nights into days . . .

And Bidhu daroga smiles. Well, not exactly
smiles. But a smile dances on the tip of his
moustache, and a ray of light darts in his eyes,
and his stomach shakes silently, and his nose
twitches, and his ears quiver like the wings of a
dragonfly. He does not *smile*. But it is still a
smile.

Translated by Abhijit Gupta

The Thief

Potash's father, Naba, was a famous thief, as was Naba's father, Bhaba. The family had been thieves for three generations. Bhaba was the most famous thief of his time. People still remember how he stole his aunt's prayer mat one afternoon. The task was not as easy as it sounds, for his aunt had been sitting on the mat embroidering a quilt when the theft took place. His aunt had shed tears of joy and blessed her nephew: 'O Bhaba, such talent is surely a gift from the good lord above. You should never give it up.'

Thanks to his aunt's blessings, Bhaba did not give it up. In time, he trained his son Naba in everything that he knew. Naba did not do too badly either. It is not easy to train as a thief. One has to learn to run fast, jump heights as well as lengths, vault walls with a bamboo pole, and cover long distances on stilts. One has to have a strong physique as well, and be prepared to fight one's way through. Then there is the small business of being skilled in acting and social niceties, for it would be a disaster if a thief were to be recognised as one. Now not only was Naba skilled in all these, he was also fearless. Lifting two maunds of iron or taking on wrestlers was nothing to him, and he was also well versed in the casting of spells. He could cast spells which would send guard dogs to sleep while he went about his thieving. On one occasion, he had managed to steal a paan from the house of the zamindar Tarini Ray. Again, this was by no means as easy as it sounds. The occasion was the rice-eating ceremony of the zamindar's grandson, and the house was full of guests who had just stuffed themselves on a particularly lavish luncheon. Bipin *khuro*, an uncle of Ray moshai, had just picked out a special Benarasi paan from his silver case and was about to transfer it to his mouth, when the unbelievable happened. The paan was stolen! For a few moments, the theft did not quite register with Bipin *khuro* who was still wondering how the paan he had just held in his two fingers had suddenly gone missing. In fact, he chewed on thin air for a few moments before realising that it was not the paan but his own tongue that he was chewing. In the meantime, the real paan was in Naba's mouth.

After this incident, Tarini Ray offered to make Naba his court thief, just as there were court poets and court jesters in olden days. Naba had, however, declined. With folded hands he had told Ray moshai, 'It would not be right to give up my family trade.'

'You don't need to give it up!' Ray moshai had argued. 'You will be able to practise your calling to your heart's content. A thief you will be, but for pleasure not profit.'

But Naba would not be prevailed upon and Ray moshai did not press him too much either, but gave him a gold medal for his pains. He always had a soft spot for Naba.

Such was Naba, whose son was Potash. Potash was a complete good-for-nothing. He seemed to know everything, but something was missing. His father had taught him all the tricks of the trade, and Potash had been quite an able learner. He could run like a deer, jump like a monkey, and was as strong as an elephant. He was not lacking in wits either. Despite all this though, he had no real interest in stealing. He learnt all that his father taught him, but his mind was not in it.

On one occasion, Naba sent Potash on practice stealing to the house of Akshay Hajra, the moneylender. Potash got there all right, but then began to do all the things that a thief should not do. All four of Hajra's guard dogs knew Potash well, so they did not attack him and fell silent after a bark or two. This did not please Potash at all. He threw stones at the dogs till they set up an unholy ruckus. Then he created a din fit to wake the dead while unpicking the door lock. Not content with all this, he began to hum a tune under his breath.

Akshay Hajra lived in constant fear, what with all the money and jewellery stashed in his house. Potash's humming woke him up, and he yelled, 'Who is there? Who, who?'

'I am Potash.'

'Potash? What now? I can't open the door at this time of the night. If you want to pawn something, give it to me through the window. Here, put it in my hand.'

'That will not be necessary. I have already broken the door.'

'Broken the door? What on earth are you up to?'

'I came to steal.'

'To steal! Is this a joke? Is this any way to steal? Out, out, get out of my sight!'

The next morning, Akshay Hajra told the whole story to Naba. 'What kind of son have you raised, Naba? You were a thief as well, but you did not make a racket or swagger about. Do you know what this son of yours has done? When I asked him what he was doing, he said nonchalantly that he had come to steal. He was humming some song as well. What is the world coming to, Naba?'

That day, Naba thrashed Potash black and blue with his slippers. But even as he handed out the thrashing, he realised that nothing would come of Potash. It would be the end of the family trade.

Potash was indifferent to all this. He ate, drank and was his usual self. Sometimes he deigned to assist his father in his work but would be more of a hindrance than help. Once he dropped the crowbar with a clang; another time he thought he saw a snake and started shouting. On one outing, Naba was hard at work opening safes and cupboards, when Potash noticed an unoccupied bed. He lay down on the bed and immediately fell asleep. Now Naba had no idea that Potash might possibly be among the sleepers, so when he could not find his son, he returned home alone.

In the morning, a yawning Potash turned up on the doorstep. Naba gave him one slap and asked, 'Where were you?'

'I fell asleep.'

'Fell asleep, you scoundrel? Call yourself a thief's son?'

'What to do? I was feeling terribly sleepy.'

'I hope they gave you a good thrashing at least.'

'Why should they? Not after I told them everything.'

'Everything? What do you mean, everything?'

'I told them the truth. That I had come to steal with my father and fell asleep. I told them your name as well. Then they gave me breakfast.'

'They gave you what?'

'Breakfast. And why not, after I had given them such a tip about the theft? They are all coming with sticks.'

Clutching his head, Naba fell to the ground.

That very day, Naba threw Potash out of his house. He went around saying, 'From today, Potash is no longer my son.'

No one knew where Potash went.

In time, Naba grew old. His teeth fell out, his hair turned white and he began to lose his sight and strength. His judgment became clouded, and he was no longer the daredevil that he used to be. It became increasingly hard to carry on the family business. Earlier, he would go out stealing every night but this was no longer possible. He turned to his savings and started a line in money-lending. This proved to be a profitable venture, and Naba gradually turned into a miser.

After being thrown out of his house, at first Potash had been all at sea. He found it hard to get work as Naba had taught him only to steal. There was no longer good food to be had, and he began to grow thin. Then he found work as a servant in a household, washing, fetching and cleaning. Things went well for a while but suddenly, once, in the middle of the night, he felt an irresistible urge. To his great surprise, he found his hands rummaging among chests and drawers, on their own.

Potash was so terrified at this that he was about to cry thief. But he stopped himself in time. To his continuing surprise, he found himself picking locks and removing valuables with the greatest of ease. What else could this be but the call of blood? There was no getting away from it.

Potash fled the household and found work in another. But after some time, the urge seized him again and Potash sighed. He realised that though his father had not been able to make him into a working thief, he had nevertheless created a thief inside him. It had been asleep so far but now it was wide awake.

As a thief, Potash was no fool. He moved from place to place, never stopping anywhere for any length of time. He would also vary his ways of stealing. Whatever he earned by way of theft, he blew up in no time. Stealing became a compulsion with him.

One night, Potash entered a village which looked quite prosperous. There were a fair number of houses, and it was easy for Potash's practised eye to figure out which ones were worth breaking into. Finally, he chose one which looked more like a fort than a house: high walls all around, thick grilles, and doors and windows made of thick wooden planks. There was a guard dog as well. All this pleased Potash: stealing was no fun unless there was some difficulty in it.

It did not take very long for Potash to scale the walls, tie the dog's mouth, and enter the house through a window. But the moment he stepped inside, he felt that there was something familiar about the house.

In the meantime, Naba had also woken up. He could hear something, but this was not the usual noise made by cat or mice. This was something different. He sniffed the air and smelt something different as well. It dawned on a wonderstruck Naba that there was a thief in the house. A thief in a thief's house! He could hardly believe it.

In the dark, Naba reached for his stick but could not find it. He was no longer strong enough to launch himself at the thief. His left leg ached painfully at all hours. But his house was full of money and valuables. The thief would clean out everything if he didn't do something.

In a hoarse voice, Naba began to shout: 'Help, thief! Thief! Help, thief!'

Translated by Abhijit Gupta

The Burp

Darubrahma had put up his ancestral house for sale. The house had been in the family for fourteen generations and was more like a palace than a house. It was hard to find buyers for such a property, and the few who expressed interest were unwilling to pay a fair price. The property was too far in the back of beyond, they argued, for it to be worth their while. This could not be denied. However, once upon a time the village was quite a bustling town, and Darubrahma's ancestor, fourteen times removed, was the local king. The palace then had stables, a Shiva temple, an ornamental pool, audience rooms for both the nobility and the gentry, a room of mirrors, a music chamber and so on. They are currently all in a dilapidated state, including the two rusted cannons on either side of the main gate. But at last, a buyer had been found.

Darubrahma was in very dire straits. On most days he did not get two square meals. He was an only child and had not married. His father had passed on, so it should not have been difficult for him and his aged mother to scrape along. But in order to honour family customs, he had to give shelter to a bunch of good-for-nothing relatives. Darubrahma got a migraine from the unholy racket they made all day. At twenty-five, his hair had begun to turn grey from worry and lack of prospects. His aged mother had chosen a bride for Darubrahma, but the bride's father was unwilling to give his daughter's hand in marriage to such a ne'er-do-well. This had really cut Darubrahma to the quick. He was therefore quite relieved when a buyer was finally found; now if he could get fifty thousand, he would retire with his mother to Kashi.

Before the sale, Darubrahma was wandering about the house one last time. Satyabrahma, his forefather six times removed, had been a man of fierce temper. Once, on being bitten on the nose by a mosquito, he had ordered it blasted by cannons. When the cannoneer had reported that there was no powder, an undeterred Satyabrahma had called for his rifle. According to witnesses, the mosquito was finally killed after a hundred or so rounds of firing. The darbaar walls were still pock-marked with the fusillade. Darubrahma traced the holes with his fingers and sighed several times.

Then there was Purnabrahma, nine times removed and addicted to hunting. But he was not exactly the most energetic of hunters. Where others would go hunting on horseback or hunt from a machan in a forest, Purnabrahma would fall ill at the mere prospect of setting foot out of doors. So he had a terrace and an artificial forest built on the first floor of the house. A trained tiger would be tethered somewhere in the bushes. Purnabrahma would then hunt the tiger on foot and fire on sight. The tiger would obediently slump to the ground. But everyone knew that there were no bullets in the rifle, only blanks, and that the tiger was trained. The same tiger had died many times in the cause of hunting. Darubrahma gazed upon the ruins of the forest, and made the air heavy with his sighs.

Krishnabrahma, thrice removed, had been a body-builder. He worked out twice daily with a pair of two-maund dumb-bells. The dumb-bells had since occupied the landing in front of the ground-floor staircase. For a few moments, Darubrahma clasped the dumb-bells to his chest and closed his eyes in fond memory.

Most of the rooms on the third storey were locked as long as one could remember. The ceilings were cracked, and only a few windows had grilles or shutters. Bats hung from the rafters. Piles of old furniture lay rotting. Darubrahma unlocked a door and went in for one last time. The room was full of unused stuff such as cabinets, bedsteads, safes, broken chandeliers and beds, old slippers and so on.

Darubrahma opened a safe and fiddled with the things inside in a distracted manner. Suddenly, something slipped from his grasp and fell on the floor. Darubrahma started, and not without reason. There was a gleam of metal as the thing fell, and a puff of smoke. Darubrahma bent low to pick the object up. It was a lamp. As Darubrahma stood in surprise with the lamp in his hand, the puff of smoke spiralled and resolved itself into the figure of a tall, thin, scrawny-looking man.

'Who, who is that?' yelled Darubrahma.

The man yawned three or four times, snapped his fingers and said, 'Me? Oh, I guess I am the genie of the lamp.'

Darubrahma gaped in disbelief. Then he shouted again, 'Is this some kind of joke? I bet you are up to no good, you thieving good-for-nothing!'

There was fear in the man's voice: 'No no. It's just that no one's summoned me for the last thousand or so years. I've been sleeping all the while. I know nothing about any theft, sir.'

Darubrahma was not a man who took fright

easily. After all, he came from a family known for its courage. He realised that the man was not pulling a fast one. His family had accumulated many curiosities over the years, and the magic lamp of Aladin could well be one among them. He said, 'Hmm. So what is it that you do?'

The man yawned a few more times, and said despondently, 'Well, I don't do much, do I? I was just having a quiet little nap, and you had to wake me up. I suppose I'll now have to do whatever you ask me. All right, but don't ask me to do anything strenuous straightaway. I'm still a bit drowsy.'

Darubrahma was now sure that this was indeed Aladin's genie, but a slippery customer if ever there was one. He said sharply, 'Don't give yourself such airs. I know all about you. You are supposed to perform feats of great labour. Can you deny that?'

The man said, even more despondently, 'That I did. But I haven't had practice for a long time. And though I've been resting, it's not as if I've had anything to eat. No food for one thousand five hundred years! It's a wonder I haven't wasted away. How about a light snack, sir?'

'And what then?'

'Well, I could try doing some of those feats of labour.'

Darubrahma was not a heartless man. He felt a bit sorry for the starving genie. He said, 'Alright, let's see if I can get you some *muri*,' and went downstairs with the genie. None of the people in the house paid them any attention. Not that there was anything to pay attention to. Darubrahma took the genie to his room and gave him a basin of *muri-batasha*. The genie washed it down with a tumbler of water and sighed, 'What's cooking for the evening? This is not even going to produce a tiny burp.'

Darubrahma also sighed. 'There was a time when dinner-guests left a tribute of gold after a meal in our house. But those days are gone. You'd be lucky to get some rice and dal.'

'Just rice and dal?' The genie was genuinely dismayed.

Darubrahma laughed. 'Just look at you. As the genie of the lamp, *you* are the one supposed to bring food, not ask for it, you know.'

Without replying, the genie turned back into a wisp of smoke and disappeared inside the lamp. After dinner, Darubrahma tapped the lamp and summoned the genie, who immediately polished off enough food for four. Then, turning to Darubrahma, he solemnly announced, 'I happen to be a heavy eater. Though I don't mind not eating a bellyful, surely a burp is not too much to expect? But this is really too little. Anyway, time for bed.' The genie yawned once, and disappeared inside his lamp.

The following day, the genie exhausted Darubrahma's entire stock of rice at one go. Darubrahma did not mind much and in fact felt sorry for the long-starving genie. He reasoned that sooner or later, he would realise all this with compound interest from the genie—in the meantime why not let him have a few square meals.

Rummaging among his papers, Darubrahma found some old title deeds which gave his family ownership of the Chowmari plots by the river. But no dues had been collected from them in recent memory. He also found deeds to a part-share in an oil-mill. Then there was a whole tehsil which he had never even heard of. Armed with a battered umbrella, Darubrahma set off in search of his lost property. He looked up the numbers of his plots and after much search, managed to locate them. His tenants were a bit hostile in the beginning, but then admitted that they hadn't paid any dues or share of crop in a very long time. Darubrahma was trying to wheedle something out of them when their headman turned up. Wiping a tear from his eyes, he said, 'The goddess has deserted us ever since we started depriving the landlord of his just share. You go along, good sir, we will not be found wanting this time.'

Darubrahma then made his way to the oil-mill and found it flourishing. He went up to the mill-owner and presented his claim. The owner fainted. When he came to, he said, 'It seems that you own two-thirds of the mill—that hardly leaves me with anything. I had no idea of this, all this was well before my time. Anyway, let me see what I can do. You go along now, sir.'

The visit to the tehsil also proved fruitful. The tenants said, 'We never for a moment imagined that there was an owner somewhere. But we are not ungrateful, we will make it up to you.'

A couple of days later, Darubrahma came back home to find four bullock carts parked outside his house. They were laden with pulses, spices and groceries, as well as two jars full of coins. That day, Darubrahma cooked for ten extra people and summoned the genie of the lamp. 'Eat, eat to your heart's content,' he said. 'My ancestors will curse me from above if they hear that I have let my dinner guests leave without burping.'

But there was no burp. The genie polished off the dinner for ten and said dolefully, 'That's it?'

Darubrahma gaped at him in amazement.

At night, the genie ate enough for a score of people, but there was no burp. Within a week, he had eaten his way through all four cartloads. By then, everyone in the house had come to know that the genie was unable to burp despite eating such huge quantities. Every day during mealtimes, they would crowd around and wait for the genie to burp. But the burp never came. However, such heavy eating soon turned the meagre-looking genie into a gargantuan figure. He became as tall as a palm tree. His arms were like clubs, his chest was like a piece of wooden board, and his teeth were like radishes.

But Darubrahma was not one to give up. He found it intolerable that a family as noble as his could not get so much as a burp out of a common genie. There was a time when guests were not able to rise for two full days after a feast given by his family. Some even went to their heavenly abode in the process. What an insult to such a house!

Darubrahma became obsessed with collecting

unpaid dues. He took over the running of the oil-mill himself and started new businesses. Cartloads of rice, sacks of vegetables, milk, curd, butter, kept arriving at his doorstep. Soon, he would realise all these manifold from the genie. Just let him burp once!

In the meantime, a buyer had turned up for the house. It was lunchtime, and Darubrahma had just summoned the genie. At this sight, the buyer fainted and fell off his chair. He had not turned up since. But Darubrahma was no longer interested in selling the house. It did not make sense anyway. Thanks to the magic lamp, he need never be in hardship again. What was the point in selling family property? He called in contractors and started making repairs to the house, secure in the belief that one day all this would be recouped from the genie.

Darubrahma acquired some more freehold land, and started farming on it. His businesses flourished. Now he had cattle in the sheds, horses in the stables, and a carriage parked in front of his house. The garden, after years of neglect, began to flower again. The house gleamed after acquiring new coats of paint. The unwilling father of the bride now came around with folded hands and said, 'I will be honoured if you accept my daughter's hand in marriage.' And so he did. Shehnai players played at Darubrahma's wedding, and guests from seven villages ate to their heart's content.

But the genie still did not burp, not even after eating as much as the seven villages put together. However he did admit, 'The hunger has gone away a bit, my stomach does not feel completely empty any more,' and then promptly went off to sleep. Darubrahma turned scarlet with shame at this insult in front of his newly-wedded wife. After all, he was a millionaire now. It was unthinkable that he could not satisfy a genie's hunger. He redoubled his exertions the very next day.

About a month later, Darubrahma threw a feast for about a hundred villagers and invited the genie to it. The genie, who was by now gigantic, took his place with a very embarrassed air. He had hardly taken a mouthful or two of rice when a sudden noise like a thunderclap startled everyone out of their wits. Ka-boom! Ka-boom! Ka-boom! Three times in a row! Complete pandemonium broke out, with everyone shouting and yelling. Children clapped their hands and danced up and down: at last, at last, the genie has burped at last!

The genie rose from his seat, his head bowed. After ablutions, he was about to re-enter his lamp when Darubrahma stopped him. 'Not so fast, my dear genie. I have waited long for this day. Now that you have finally burped, it's time to deliver, don't you think?' The genie stared at him in some amazement. 'Of course I will have to do your bidding, if you so desire. But what is there left for me to do? Most people I meet ask me for wealth and riches, and I carry out their wishes. But just look around you—do you really want me to bring more riches on top of all this?'

This had not occurred to Darubrahma before.

He looked around. The genie was right. There was really no point in asking for anything more. He scratched his head: 'That's true, but . . . ' The genie made a doleful face and said, 'There cannot be anything lacking in a house where I have eaten and burped. Is it very necessary to put me to work again? I wouldn't mind going back to sleep for a couple of thousand years. Feeling a bit fatigued, y'know.'

Darubrahma sighed. 'So be it,' he said.

The genie vanished into the lamp. Darubrahma picked it up and locked it carefully into his safe.

Translated by Abhijit Gupta

Trouble at the Well

There was only one well in the village from which good water could be had. The water was as sweet as it was clear. Anyone who had a drink from the well would even find iron digestible.

The story about digesting iron was not at all a tall tale. Ramu the conjuror had once been performing at the Gobindapur fair. One of his tricks was swallowing real nails, and then bringing them up again. Actually, he did not swallow them—he merely pretended to, and tucked them away under his tongue or in his cheek.

However, Ramu was no longer the conjuror that he once was. He had grown old and lost some of his teeth, while the others were not too strong either. So he had some artificial teeth made from the city. But the real and the false teeth were constantly gnashing against each other, creating great confusion. The two sets of teeth did not get along at all. On one occasion, Ramu had even started gnawing on some of his false teeth, mistaking them for bones. Anyway, that's another story.

So here was Ramu, with his mouth full of mismatched teeth, about to land into trouble as he prepared to do his swallowing trick. As usual, he had drunk a glass of water along with the nails and was holding forth: 'Nails? Nails are easy, I could even swallow the Howrah bridge if I wanted. In fact, I had once set out to do so. But the government got wind of my plan and nearly threw me into jail. I just about managed to escape.'

As he spoke, he prepared to gag and throw up as usual, when he suddenly realised that there were no nails in his mouth. They had been washed into his stomach along with the water.

Ramu almost fainted in panic when he understood what had happened. Nearly a dozen nails in his stomach—it was no joke. Within half an hour, Ramu began to foam at the mouth and writhe with stomach pains. The apothecary pronounced his diagnosis, 'Ruptured intestine, perforated stomach, leaky food canal, lungs collapsed like a balloon losing its air: there is no hope.'

Then someone had a brainwave, 'Give him water from the old well.'

Ramu sat up within half an hour of drinking a pint of water from the well. So it was really a case of being able to digest iron.

The well was already quite famous, but after this incident, it became even more so. In fact, the villagers of Gobindapur who drank from the well did not suffer a day's illness.

But something had gone wrong of late. Every time you lowered a bucket or a pot into the well, the rope would break. Well, most of the time the rope would break, but on other occasions, someone would have carefully untied the rope from the bucket handle. There was no way you could lift water. The same thing would happen every time you lowered a bucket with a rope.

The villagers went in a body to their priest, and said, 'Thakur moshai, you must do something.'

The priest had been sitting with his head in his hands. He said dolefully, 'Forget ropes, I even tried using an iron chain for the bucket, but that snapped as well. And on top of that, there was great turmoil in the water. Have any of you seen waves in a well, rising like the sea? Well, I did, yesterday evening, with my own eyes. I think it best that we don't drink from that well any more.'

Now Harihar Ray was the zamindar of five villages. He was a good, gentle, god-fearing man, who cared for his subjects. The villagers of Gobindapur decided to go to him for redress.

Ray moshai sat in his kutchery, a small court, a fair, roly-poly figure of a man. His *nayeb* moshai or manager came up to him, scratched his head and said, 'There is a delegation from Gobindapur with a petition.'

Despite being a very gentle soul, Ray moshai

could rage and roar like a tiger. He could be quite fearsome if he lost his temper. And he was not at all pleased with the villagers of Gobindapur. During the wedding of his second son, when his other subjects gave gifts of gold or jewellery, the rascally villagers of Gobindapur had turned up with a milch cow. They had dragged the cow on a leash and handed one end of the rope to the newly-wedded bride, beaming all the while.

Ray moshai had taken great offense at this. It was not as if the cow was bad or anything—in fact, it was the best cow he had. She gave as much as seven seers of milk twice a day. And what milk—as thick as the gum of the banyan tree, and sweet beyond compare. But Ray moshai could not forget the embarrassment caused by the cow being brought to the wedding. He would still hang his head in shame when he thought of it; or else, he would turn red with rage.

So when Ray moshai heard that the people of Gobindapur had come with a petition, he let loose a terrific roar: 'What, what do they want?'

Shaken by the roar, the *nayeb* retreated a few steps, while all present sweated in panic; Ray moshai himself felt his waistband come loose with the effort.

Among the Gobindapur delegation, Chakkotti moshai the priest was a stalwart. He habitually sucked a *hortuki* at all times. This day was no exception, but the zamindar's sudden roar had startled him, and he had swallowed nervously to regain his composure. But then he realised that he had swallowed the *hortuki* whole in the process.

This was worrying—would Chakkotti moshai be able to digest a whole *hortuki*? There was a time when one could swallow a whole ship without worries. All one needed to do was to gulp down a pint of the well water and the ship would turn to rust. There was the time when Chakkotti moshai had eaten two buckets of golden moong dal cooked with fish-heads at a feast for Brahmins in Sonargram. Then at the funeral of Sadi pishi, he had eaten a whole goat and a half; likewise, eighty pieces of *pona* fish, two large pots of yoghurt and two seers of rosogolla at the wedding of the zamindar's second son. In fact, all the villagers of Gobindapur were known for their eating prowess: there would be a famine-like situation wherever they ate. And among these food-loving people, Chakkotti moshai was the champion eater. All this was owing to the healthful qualities of the water of the old well. One drink was all it took: your stomach would clamour in hunger in no time.

But now there was trouble at the well. In the meantime, Chakkotti moshai became extremely worried on swallowing the *hortuki*. Being a medicinal fruit, the *hortuki* was beneficial to health . . . But was it healthy to swallow a whole one? None of this would have mattered had he been able to drink from the water of the old well.

Chakkotti moshai stood with folded hands and said, 'Sire, you must have heard of the famous old well of Gobindapur. Thanks to its waters, we have never had any illness in our village. But alas, we can no longer lift water from the well.'

Ray moshai allowed himself a sardonic smile and said, 'Are you surprised? Just desserts for your sins! Who insulted me by bringing a cow to my son's wedding?'

Chakkotti moshai bit his tongue in shame and said, 'How could we ever insult you, sire? Such a thought would not cross our minds even in death. Besides, no scriptures say that it is a sin to gift cows to Brahmins. Cow-giving is a pious act.'

The court pundit, Keshab Bhattacharya, nodded his head in agreement. 'The point is moot, but admissible,' he pronounced.

Ray moshai softened a bit and said, 'I too have heard of this famous well of Gobindapur. I was once given a drink of its water and it did me great good. So what is wrong, has the well dried up?'

Chakkotti moshai took out another *hortuki* from his waistband and popped it into this mouth. 'Not exactly, sire,' he said, 'The water is as clear and tranquil as ever. But we have no way of getting at it. Nothing that is lowered into the well comes out of it. Something or someone breaks the rope every time. Even iron chains have been snapped.'

Ray moshai roared, his eyes red with anger, 'Who dares do such a thing?'

The people of Gobindapur were pleased at the zamindar's response. A ripple of excitement went through them. It was unthinkable that the waters of the well would be lost with such a zamindar watching over them.

The priest said, 'Sire, this is no human doing. No one would have such audacity. The stick-wielding men of Gobindapur are feared all over. And there is you, like salt on a wound, sire. If our stick-wielding-men fail, surely you will administer the rod of correction. But these are not human acts. These are done by spirits.'

Ray moshai had been about to lose his cool at being compared to salt on a wound, but the moment he heard the word spirits, he clapped both his ears with his hands and wailed, 'Stop stop, don't say that word.'

Everyone stared in astonishment.

The *nayeb* glared fiercely at the Gobindapur delegation and said, 'Mind your language!'

Chakkotti moshai stopped himself from swallowing the second *hortuki* with great difficulty.

Ray moshai was scared stiff of ghosts. As a rule, he never took their name, nor suffered it to be said in his presence. But curiosity prevailed in the end. After keeping his ears covered for a while, he relaxed his grip a tiny bit, and asked cautiously, 'What was that you said?'

With renewed enthusiasm, Chakkotti moshai began, 'It is a most ghostly business. Gho . . .'

'Stop I say, stop! Didn't you hear what I said?' Ray moshai clapped his ears again.

Chakkotti moshai looked about in total incomprehension. People stared at each other's faces. The *nayeb* let loose a stentorian, 'Shut up!'

After a while, Ray moshai gingerly removed one hand from an ear and asked, 'What is there in the well?'

This time Chakkotti moshai spoke with

some hesitation, 'Sire, it seems to be poltergeist activity . . .'

'Hold you tongue, hold you tongue. Ram Ram Ram Ram,' the zamindar chanted.

His hands were back at his ears. After a few moments, he looked at the villagers with glassy eyes and said, 'Tell me, but carefully.'

'Sire, the . . . they snap the ropes of pots and buckets. Even chains. There is no breeze or wind inside the well, but there are waves as tall as palm trees, and the water swirls and swells.'

'Ohoho,' the zamindar shuddered and closed his eyes.

Eventually, Ray moshai was able to hear the whole story. Then he sighed, 'You have ruined the day for me. *Nayeb* moshai, please station four sentries in my bedroom tonight.'

'It will be done.'

The villagers from Gobindapur said with folded hands, 'Sire, now that you have arranged sentries for yourself, could you please do something for our well?'

'Best seal it. I don't think it is wise to use it any more. If you want, I can send over a few cartloads of good soil.'

Not just the villagers from Gobindapur, but everyone present at the *kutchery* broke out in voluble protest. 'That cannot be, sire, the water of the well is the panacea for all our ailments. And there is nothing wrong with the water, no pestilence or anything, just a few gho . . .'

Ray moshai bellowed, 'Shut up! Anyone who takes that name will be buried alive!'

Everyone fell silent. Ray moshai made a glum face and thought for a few moments. Then he turned to Bhattacharya moshai and said, 'This is not a job for the stick-wielding men. Do you think you should go there once?'

The previous pundit at the court, Mukunda Sharma, was still alive, but was past hundred years in age. He had become somewhat frail, and forgetful, and also demanded to eat at all hours. He was no longer of much use. So Keshab Bhattacharya had been appointed as the new court pundit.

Keshab was not a native of the region. He had been brought from Kashi. As such, his powers and scholarship were still untested. However, his appearance commanded respect. He was a strapping figure of a man, and of radiant complexion, but that was not what mattered. His face gave the impression that there was something in him which went beyond physical appearances. It was personality.

Keshab smiled briefly at the zamindar's words.

The next morning, Keshab set off towards Gobindapur on a bullock-cart. Following him on foot were nearly two hundred villagers of Gobindapur.

Keshab reached the village by afternoon and rested awhile in the headman's house. Then he set off for the well. The crowd had swelled to thousands by then, from Gobindapur as well as neighbouring villages.

The well had been dug at a charming spot. There were bowers of *kolke* flowers and hibiscus all around, and a huge peepul tree cast its shadow on the well. Birds cooed and butterflies flitted about.

Keshab walked up slowly to the side of the well. His face was grave. He leaned towards the water. It was really transparent and crystal-clear. Keshab said softly, 'Is there anyone there? Come up, or I will spit.'

No one knew how it happened, but all of a sudden there was pandemonium within the well. Massive waves surged as high as the edge of the well, and there was the scything sounds of a powerful wind.

Everyone who had gathered by the well ran to a safe distance. Only Chakkotti moshai stood his ground, though he trembled in fear.

'Don't spit, please don't spit,' hundreds of ghosts wailed as they began to emerge from the well. They did not look fearsome at all. They were stick-thin and black, and did not have any flesh and blood but were made of some kind of shadowy substance. They were all dripping wet, and water dripped from their hair.

Keshab regarded them gravely and asked, 'What were you doing in there?'

'Sir, the number of ghosts in this region has been falling sharply. Thanks to the water of the well, there is no sickness in the village. People are living for a hundred, hundred and fifty years. How will there be any more ghosts if people stop dying? That is why we thought of occupying the well.'

Then the ghosts scratched their heads.

Keshab observed, 'A very moot point. But it is admissible.'

Encouraged, the ghosts said, 'Well, look at Chakkotti moshai there. He is at least one hundred and twenty years old. Ask him if you don't believe us.'

Keshab looked in surprise at Chakkoti and said, 'Is it true what they say?'

Chakkotti moshai, who was fingering his sacred thread with one hand, and reciting the *Gayatri mantra* with the other, stammered in reply, 'I-I don't remember very clearly.'

'A moot point, but admissible,' said Keshab.

At this point, a very moot point also occurred to Chakkotti. He asked, 'Do ghosts die?'

'That is also a moot point,' Keshab said thoughtfully.

Immediately Chakkotti said, 'But admissible. It doesn't look very good if ghosts don't die at all. The poet Michael has sung: "We live to die, man is mortal / there is nothing called life eternal."'

The ghosts howled in unison, 'What do we do then? We don't have heart attacks, malaria, cholera, cerebral attacks or brain fever—then how will we die? Is it our fault that we cannot die?'

Chakkotti, who had mustered up some courage by then, said, 'But the fault is not on our side either, you know.'

Keshab observed, 'This is a very moot point indeed.'

Chakkotti added, 'But admissible.'

Nearly five hundred grotesque, bedraggled and very wet ghosts looked at Keshab in great anxiety, waiting for his ruling.

A senior ghost broke into tears and said, 'Thakur moshai, just as rice ferments from being in water, we have also become fermented ghosts from spending so much time inside the well. We have put in a lot of work in the cause of increasing our numbers, please do not let our labour go waste.'

'This is also a very moot point,' said Keshab.

This time Chakkotti moshai did not add 'But admissible'. Summoning up new reserves of courage, he ventured, 'In that case, there should be some rules about the death of ghosts as well. If there aren't any, then I will also spit into the well. But why go so far? I could just as well spit on you from where I am standing.'

By now, Chakkotti moshai had figured out that the ghosts were mortally scared of spit. As soon as he had finished speaking, the ghosts leapt back nearly ten feet and started screaming, 'Don't spit, we beg of you. Don't spit.'

Keshab restrained Chakkotti moshai with one hand, and turned to the ghosts. 'The point which Chakkotti moshai has raised is a moot one, and also admissible. On the other hand, there is some merit in your argument as well. Now, logically speaking, ghosts do not die, so there is no subtraction in their number, only addition. On the other hand, human beings do die eventually, even though they might live as long as two hundred years. So the number of human beings does get reduced. Therefore, your argument does not hold water.'

The ghosts continued to wail in protest, 'We have put in a lot of hard work . . .'

'No,' said Keshab firmly, 'that cannot be. You must return all the pots and pans which have sunk to the bottom, and then leave the well. If you don't Chakkotti moshai and I will both spi . . .'

He did not have to say any more. The ghosts began diving into the well and bringing up pots and buckets with a clatter. Within seconds the sides of the well were high with pots and buckets.

From then on, the old well ceased to be haunted by ghosts. The ghosts spent the next few days lying on the fields of Gobindapur, drying themselves in the sun. In their dried-up state, they looked even more emaciated. Eventually, they became so thin that even the children of the village ceased to be afraid of them.

Translated by Abhijit Gupta

Haro Babu the Gentleman

Haro babu sensed that a burglar had entered his house. So he sat up on his bed and murmured, 'This is outrageous behaviour!'

Very irritated, he got up from his bed. He opened the door of his room, went out onto the balcony, and gazed at the moonlight quietly. He disliked burglary very much. It was not possible for him to stand the sight of a burglar robbing his house under his own nose.

The burglar was quite shameless. He was not even trying to hide the sinful act that he was engaged in. From the balcony, Haro babu could hear horrible noises of boxes being moved, utensils falling, cupboards being broken in.

Angrily, he turned his face towards the room and shouted, 'Not so loud! Shameless idiot!'

The thief, or maybe the thieves, took the hint and refrained from making loud noises. But it was taking ages for them to finish their act. The burglars these days were mere novices. They would not learn their trade properly, and get to work only after a few days of training.

Haro babu stood gazing at the moonlit night. After about an hour, there came a voice that was naturally rough, but was sweetened for the occasion to the extent possible: 'My work is done, sir. You can now go to sleep.'

Haro babu stood up, yawned, walked to his room and lay down on his bed. The thieves these days had become very greedy and discourteous. They had taken the bedsheet, the flashlight that he kept beside his pillow, everything. He had kept some water in a metal glass so that he could drink it at night. Even that glass had vanished.

The thief had taken everything. So now, Haro babu would have to go to the vegetable market, to cook, and to eat. Haro babu borrowed some money and set out for the market.

The potato seller, the *patol* seller, the fish seller, they all knew Haro babu quite well. Even on days when Haro babu had no need for potatoes, the potato seller would catch him and pour two kilograms of potatoes into his bag. Haro babu did not eat *jhinge* or bitter gourds, but that was no excuse for the people who sold those things. He had to buy a kilogram of those vegetables almost everyday. They rotted at home. Haro babu murmured to himself, 'All vegetable sellers are robbers and rogues.'

Haro babu was on the way to the market with borrowed money when he met Khalifa Haldar.

'Hello Haro, what do you want to do about the hundred rupees that you borrowed from me three months ago?'

Haro babu looked absolutely grief-stricken. It was true that about three months ago he had borrowed one hundred rupees from Khalifa Haldar. But Haro babu also clearly remembered that he had returned the money one month after that. And because Khalifa babu did not remember the latter incident, Haro babu had to pay the money back again the following month. Haro babu took even that in good humour. Anybody can make mistakes. However, when last month Khalifa asked again for the money to be returned, Haro babu was irritated, but paid the money back again. And now Khalifa was asking for the money one more time!

Haro babu heaved a sigh and asked very hesitantly, 'Haven't I given the money back to you?'

'Have you? Now, when did you do that? At least I cannot remember.'

Haro babu lowered his gaze and said in a tone mixed with shame, 'Oh, then I should give it back to you. Alright. I will do it in the next couple of days.'

Haro babu always bought things from the grocery store on credit. The grocer told Haro babu, 'Please check your bill. Last month, you bought things worth one hundred and seventy two rupees and eighty two paise.'

Haro babu heaved another sigh. He also had a notebook where he jotted down the transactions at the grocery store. According to his own accounts, the amount should have been sixty two rupees and fifteen paise. But it gave him a lot of pain to say things bluntly to someone.

So he said, 'Okay, I will pay the bill. Give me a couple of days.'

He had a lot of trouble cooking and eating that day. The utensils were all gone, so he had bought an earthen pot and banana leaves. He barely managed to cook rice and boil vegetables in the earthen pot and then served the food for himself on a banana leaf. After eating, he started walking to the school where he taught mathematics.

The roadsides and the marketplaces were teeming with beggars. These days, beggars were also very fastidious. Most people did not give any alms, and whoever gave something gave very little. But Haro babu was a different story. The beggars' eyes lit up as soon as they spotted Haro babu. If he gave five or ten paise, the beggars felt quite offended. Once Haro babu gave only ten paise to an old beggar. He was disgusted, gave the money back to Haro babu, and said, 'Only ten paise! What do you think, are we beggars?'

So Haro babu had to shell out a quarter or half a rupee. The beggars, not satisfied, kept asking for one rupee or two. Haro babu got angry, but what could he say?

And the students at school, were they any better?

Before Haro babu reached the classroom, students of class six created a huge ruckus. Some of them were reading story books, some playing tic-tac-toe, some others were screaming at the top of their voice, some were loitering outside the classroom.

When Haro babu entered the classroom, the chaos increased by a factor of two. There were fist-fights, there was shouting. Some boys had rolled some paper into the form of a ball and were playing football at the back of the room where there was some empty space. Some of them left the room, without even bothering to take Haro babu's permission, to drink water or to go to the restroom.

Haro babu did not pay any attention to any of these. He wrote a math problem on the blackboard and meekly told the class, 'Be quiet and solve it.'

Nobody paid any heed to these words. Haro babu got irritated, and stared out through the open door. He had no clue why the students made such a racket. After some time, he got up from his chair, wrote down the solution on the blackboard, and said, 'Copy it down.'

No one did.

Haro babu never hit any student, never scolded any, and never gave pompous advice to anyone. During the exams, it was a feast for the students who sat in the classroom where he was given the invigilation duty. So far Haro babu had never caught anyone copying in the exam. If he saw anyone doing such a thing, he turned his head immediately and looked in a different direction.

Other teachers made fun of Haro babu. Haro

babu listened to everything silently, with a smile on his face, never protesting to anything that was said of him. Secretly, many of the teachers also borrowed money from him. If they did not pay him back, Haro babu could not tell them anything about the matter.

While returning from school, Haro babu came face to face with a huge ox in the narrow road of the Kali temple. He moved to the side and leaned against a wall. And yet, the scoundrel ox shook its horns when it came near Haro babu, as if to share a joke. One horn hit his right ribs. Haro babu groaned in pain, but could not say anything to the ox.

When he was passing by the pond surrounded by palm trees, a dog stormed towards him in a very impolite manner, gnashing its teeth. Haro babu just turned his head and walked along. He did not admonish the dog at all.

When evening fell, Haro babu went out for a walk. This had been part of his daily routine for a long time.

He started walking aimlessly and found himself near the desolate river bank. The moon was gleaming brightly. The sky seemed immense, and so did the solitude. He felt overwhelmed by the happiness and peace all around him.

Just then, a big, rough-looking man stepped in front of him and said, 'Give me all you have got with you.'

The man had a big knife in his hand. Haro babu got really irritated. He really got mad if someone spoiled the tranquility of his evenings.

In fact, he did not even have anything worth handing over to this man. His house had been robbed last night. Haro babu told the man meekly, 'I am giving you whatever I have, but don't make a noise. Noise, in these circumstances, bothers me very much.'

Saying this, Haro babu took out whatever money he had in his pocket and gave it to the man. The man probably sensed something about Haro babu and did not press for more, just took the pen from his pocket before leaving. Good riddance!

Haro babu took a new plunge in the deep ocean of happiness around him.

Time was flowing by nicely. Suddenly, from a distance, he heard someone screaming, 'Help me, help me, or this guy will kill me!'

Haro babu was very displeased by the interruption of his enjoyment of the tranquility. What was this? Couldn't one spend some time sitting quietly in the beautiful moonlight?

At first, he did nothing. But then there was another scream in a woman's voice, 'Help me! Help me!' And there was a man's harsh voice threatening, 'Shut up, or I will kill you.'

That was quite unbearable. It was a disquieting thought that one could not spend some time sitting quietly somewhere. So Haro babu got up.

He crossed the little hillock of the firing range and saw a couple standing there helplessly with a child. It seemed that they also had been out for a walk. In front of them, the big and rough man was brandishing his knife.

Haro babu gnashed his teeth and said to himself,

'If you have to mug people, that's your business. But why do you have to make a noise and disturb the peace? Why do you have to spoil this quiet evening of beautiful milky moonlight? Why won't you let others enjoy happiness?'

Haro babu walked up to the guy and shouted at him, 'Who do you think you are? What is going on? Didn't I tell you once not to make any noise?'

The man pointed his knife at him and said, 'Get lost if you want to stay alive.'

'What! You are still shouting? Making more noise?' While saying this, Haro babu placed a huge slap on the man's cheek. The man got completely disoriented with the slap.

But Haro babu's anger did not subside. He slapped him again. The knife dropped from the man's hand. He covered his cheeks with his hands, squatted, and started crying loudly.

Haro babu became more angry at the sight. 'What audacity! You are getting beaten for making a noise, and you are making more noise after that?'

He pulled the man by his shirt collar, showered him with punches and smacks and jabs and slaps, dragged him to the side of the main road, left him there, and warned, 'If you come back near the riverside, I will kill you.'

Then he returned to where he was, and with a smile on his face, started enjoying the mystery of the moonlit night.

Translated by Palash Baran Pal

The Smell is Very Suspicious

Once, my grandmother landed in big trouble. My grandfather used to work in the railways. That must have been at least fifty years ago. My mother was just a little girl at that time. There weren't very many towns and cities in those days, and not too many people either. Trees, shrubs, woods and jungles abounded. My grandfather got transferred to one such wooded place. The place was called Domohani, in north Bengal. My grandfather was a guard in freight trains, so he had to spend a lot of time away from home, sometimes three or four or even seven days at a stretch. Then he would come back home, perhaps for a day, only to leave again in another freight train. My mother had four sisters and four brothers. My grandmother used to live at home with her nine children. All of them were very young at that time, so grandma had her hands full.

Domohani was a nice and quiet place. There were short lichi trees all around. There were streets laid with stone-chips. There were green fields, and some woods. The number of people was moderate. On one side, there were brick buildings for railway officers, on another side there were brick-and-mud dwellings for railway clerks, and a school that students could attend till the eighth grade. There was also a club for railway employees where either 'Kedar Ray' or 'Tipu Sultan' was staged two or three times every year. The railway clerks used to play football in the summer and cricket in the winter. Senior officers used to come to watch the games. Sometimes, in a big group, they went for picnics near the river Tista or in the Jayantiya Hills. Though small and desolate, Domohani was a lot of fun.

Right from the time that my grandparents moved to Domohani, the older residents of that place warned them about one thing. No one said very clearly what the thing was. For example, storekeeper Akkhoy Sarkar once told my grandfather, 'Chatterjee, this place is not as good as it seems. Be careful about the people around. Don't let anyone enter your home.' Another day, Mrs. Palit from next door came and told my grandma, with a big and wry smile on her face, 'You are new here. It will take time to understand the nature of things here. Keep your eyes and ears and nose alert all the time. And be careful about the children. There are others here.'

My grandmother was frightened by the tone and asked, 'Who are you talking about?'

Mrs. Palit just said, 'Oh, there are these others. You will find out.'

Grandma started living her life under the shadow of an unknown fear.

Then once, our old maid Sukhiya got a mail from her folks, indicating that she must go back home soon, her nephew was unwell. She went away on a one-month leave. Grandma was looking for a temporary maid. Suddenly, the very next day, a middle-aged woman appeared and asked, 'Do you need a maid?'

My grandmother hesitated, but finally employed her. She worked quite well, wandered all around the house, sometimes told stories to entertain the children. About two days later, Mrs. Palit came one morning and said, 'You have a new maid now? Let me see who it is.'

Grandma stepped out of the room to call her, but found that the maid had left all the soiled pots and pans near the water tap and vanished. She called her many times, but in vain. Mrs. Palit smiled and said, 'That's how they are. Can you tell me what's the maid's name?'

Grandma said, 'Kamala.'

Mrs. Palit nodded and said, 'Yes I know her. She worked with the Haldars as well.'

Grandma was quite irritated when she said, 'Tell me clearly what it is that you want to say.'

Mrs. Palit heaved a sigh and said, 'Can all things be spelled out clearly? Anyway, that is how it is here. It is very difficult to tell which one is human and which one isn't. This time, be careful while choosing, and employ a human maid.'

Mrs. Palit left, and my grandmother started pondering about the whole thing.

Kamala came back a little later. Grandma asked her in an admonishing voice, 'Where have you been?'

She lowered her head and said meekly, 'Madam, please don't call me while other people are around. I am very shy.'

Kamala stayed. But uneasy questions remained in my Grandma's mind.

My grandfather, in turn, had a bizarre experience. One day, he went to his work in the railways. Very late in the night, the freight train was passing through the dark forest of the Duars. Grandpa was dozing in the brake van. Suddenly, the train came to a stop. Of course, that's not unusual, freight trains do such things sometimes. Some pointsman or some Assistant Station Master might fall asleep in the night, neglecting the signal for trains. It was not uncommon in those days. Grandfather thought that it was a case like that, and took out an almanac from his bag and started reading it. He was very fond of almanacs. The train was absolutely motionless. Suddenly my grandfather heard the footsteps of someone climbing to the roof of the train using the iron ladder at the back of the brake van. He stuck out his face, but could not see anyone. Then he heard the sound of some people trying to break open the wagon doors at some distance. He was really worried. Brigands sometimes disable the signals so that they can stop trains and rob goods. So Grandpa picked up his lamp and got down from the train in order to find out what was going on.

The train was quite long, with the engine up in front. By the time he walked all the way to the engine, he found that the red signal had become green, although the driver and the fireman were fast asleep on two sheets that they had spread on the pile of coals. They could not be blamed really, because they had been on duty for a long period, and were making the best use of the respite that they had got due to the unscheduled stopping of the train. Grandpa had to push them quite hard before they woke up. And then he started his journey back to the brake van, walking alongside the long train once again. He had almost reached the middle when he heard the whistle of the train, and saw that the train had started squeaking and moving. He was dumbfounded. The train was supposed to start only after he went back to the brake van and showed the green light to the driver. So my grandfather just looked on in amazement. He saw a person in the brake van, dressed exactly like the guard of a train, showing a green light to the driver. When the brake van crossed past my Grandpa, that man threw a smile at him.

My grandfather came back home after a lot of trouble.

Professor Bhattacharjee, the magician, came once to Domohani, after a show trip in the tea gardens. He used to show trivial tricks: rope-cutting, card tricks, fire-eating. Even such tricks attracted a huge number of people since Domohani was such a small place. In the beginning, Bhattacharjee gave a small lecture with a little black wand in his hand. He said that magic did not involve any supernatural power, that it was merely tricks, so if anyone understood the trick during the show, the person should please keep quiet, and no one should shine a flashlight on the stage, etc etc. While he was saying these things, before the magic started, suddenly we saw that his wand left his hand, performed a somersault in thin air, and returned slowly to the magician's hand. Everyone clapped heavily for this stunning magical feat. But Professor Bhattacharjee became very serious.

Then came the next item: any spectator could write anything on a blackboard with a chalk, and Professor Bhattacharjee, with his eyes tied up, would tell what was written. But that was not what happened on that occasion. The spectators were poking each other, trying to get the other person to walk up on to the stage, and Professor

Bhattacharjee, with his eyes covered with flour dough and a black piece of cloth, was announcing, 'Come along please, there is nothing to be afraid about, I am not a tiger or a lion' and so on. About that time, we all saw that the chalk that was lying on the table leaped off the table all by itself, sailed through the air, and wrote on the blackboard, 'Professor Bhattacharjee is the best magician of the world.' The spectators were beside themselves after seeing this extraordinary magic and went into raptures. And Bhattacharjee, his eyes still tied, made a crying face and started saying, 'What happened? Can someone tell me what happened?' And then he became even more serious.

He did something spectacular in his fire-eating game as well. It was expected that he would light up the torch, put it into his mouth and devour the fire. That was what he did. But then, whenever he opened his mouth, we could see flames coming out, wiggling like a snake's tongue. Later in the show, he was showing card tricks, and wiggly flames were still coming out of his mouth whenever he started speaking. The spectators gave him a standing ovation. But Bhattacharjee, striking a sorrowful pose, began drinking glass after glass of water right there on the stage. And yet, the flames continued to come out.

In those days, there was a practice in remote towns: if someone came to give a show in the town, the person and his associates were housed with different families for the night. Professor Bhattacharjee put up with my mother's parental family. In the night, during dinner, my grandfather told him, 'Your show is better than Ganapati's. Very very strange tricks.'

Bhattacharjee said, 'Yes, very strange tricks indeed. I have never seen such tricks myself.'

My grandfather was taken aback. He said, 'What do you mean? You are the one who showed the tricks!'

Bhattacharjee fumbled, 'That seems to be true. I showed the tricks, yes. Very strange.'

He seemed quite surprised by the whole thing.

My grandpa's father came to spend some time in Domohani. As soon as he entered the house, he said, 'Why is there such a fishy smell in the house?'

Everyone said, 'Fishy smell? Why, we didn't notice anything!'

My grandpa's father was a very religious and a very learned man. He shook his head and said, 'No, there is, definitely. Not only in your house. I felt the same smell at the station, when I got down from the train. The entire area seems to be smelling of fish.'

Kamala hid herself at the sight of my grandpa's father. She did not come out even though she was called many times. My grandmother was in trouble: she had to do everything by herself. My grandpa's father noticed everything, and commented in a very serious tone, 'This is not good. The smell is very suspicious.'

That very day, in the afternoon, Station Master Harensamaddar's mother came and told my grandmother privately, 'Kamala has taken shelter

in our house. Let me tell you this . . . I understand
that your father-in-law is a religious man, nothing
wrong with that. But if he performs prayers too
often, utters the names of gods and goddesses too
much, how can Kamala stay in your house?'

My grandmother said in a surprised tone,
'Honestly, I don't have the faintest idea what you
are talking about. What is Kamala's problem if
my father-in-law utters his prayers?'

Samaddar's mother shook my grandmother's
head by her chin, and said, 'O my God, you
mean you don't know! My child, everyone in
Domohani knows that here the others have their
ways. They are doing all the chores in all the
houses. You won't suspect a thing by just looking
at them, but they are they.'

'Who are they?'—My grandmother was still in
shock.

'Wait and see,' said Samaddar's mother, and
left.

What she said was not really untrue. There was
a dearth of maids and servants in Domohani at

that time. The entire Duars area was so infested with malaria, black fever, mosquitoes and tigers that no one wanted to be there. The only people who went there were the people who had no alternative. And, as soon as they arrived, they wanted to leave. And yet it was seen that if anyone needed some domestic help, they could always find someone.

Once my grandfather was having a chat in Station Master Samaddar's office. Samaddar was writing a letter. When he finished, he just called out, 'Is anyone around?' And immediately a young man arrived. Samaddar gave him the letter and said, 'Put it in the mail.' My grandfather said, 'Is this man a new employee?' Samaddar shook his head and said, 'Not at all. He just does some small chores. They are very nice, and come whenever they are called. Don't call them "men". They are just them.'

Well, that was how it was. In my mother's parental home, a short and pale person named Dharmadas tutored the children. On stage, he would put on women's clothes, appropriate a womanly voice and play female roles. He was so good that, seeing him on stage it was impossible to guess that he was not a woman. Once Girish Ghosh's 'Siraj-ud-daula' was staged, and he had the role of Lutfa. However, just on the day of the performance, he came down with an attack of malaria. He was in bed, groaning under a pile of quilts. The performance was about to be cancelled. But when the time came, there was no problem with Lutfa. It seemed that teacher Dharmadas, with a clean-shaven face, played the role perfectly from the beginning to the end. Nobody sensed a thing. Of course some of the insiders knew quite well that teacher Dharmadas was not on stage on that day. After the play, my grandfather was returning home with Samaddar, when the latter said, 'Did you see how nicely the problem was solved! No one even noticed the little nasal tone.'

My grandfather pressed Samaddar, 'Would you please explain to me what the mystery is?'

Samaddar laughed and said, 'You understand, I

hope. The point is that, if you are on friendly terms, you can benefit from anyone. This is a piece of advice that you should remember.'

Some of my mother's brothers who were a little older at that time used to go outside to play. My mother and her elder sister were also somewhat grown-up at that time, but her other siblings were still infants. My mother was quite addicted to the game of ludo. So, my mother and her elder sister would spread the ludo board in the afternoon and call out, 'Come!' And immediately, no one knew from where, two girls of my mother's age would appear and start playing happily with them. My two eldest uncles would go to play football. Very often, there were not enough boys in the two teams. It was a small place, there just weren't many people around. But, whenever there was a shortage, my uncles or their playmates would call, 'Who wants to play?' In a moment, four or five new players would gather around, about the same age as the boys. That made the game exciting.

Something extreme happened with football

once. There was a match between the Domohani football team and a tea-garden team. The tea-garden team came to play with some Santals and other aboriginals, all in tremendous physical shape. The Domohani team, consisting of Bengalis only, was no match for them at the beginning of the game. But then suddenly they started playing very well. They equalised the score from being down by two goals, and then scored a further goal. At this time, the captain of the tea-garden team stopped the game and told the referee, 'They are playing with twelve players.' The referee counted and found eleven only. Play resumed, but after a few minutes the referee himself stopped the game, called up Domohani's captain, and said, 'There are four or five extra people playing in your team.'

The referee was a tough Englishman, everyone was afraid of him. But Domohani's captain said nonchalantly, 'You may count and check.' The referee counted, and was stupefied to find that there were indeed eleven.

The Domohani team scored a couple of more goals. The referee stopped the game again, and shouted, 'There are at least ten extra men in this team.'

The spectators also had the same feeling. When you counted there were always just eleven, but as soon as the game started, players started coming out from the blades of grass on the field, from the air that blew. The referee lined up the entire Domohani team, looked at everyone's face carefully, and then said, 'Where are the players who scored the last three goals? How come I don't see them—a dark and lanky guy, a pale and short one, and the one who looks like a raging bull?'

Domohani's captain offered some fuzzy explanations, but that infuriated the referee even further. The tea-garden team was also completely at a loss, and quite out of breath. But no one could get to the crux of the problem.

Anyway, the game was abandoned. My grandpa's father was standing near the sideline. He watched the game for some time and said, 'The same smell here. There is a mystery here as well, won't you agree, Samaddar?'

Station Master Samaddar was just beside him. He said, 'I think they have gone a bit too far.'

'Who are they? Who are you talking about?'

Samaddar dodged the question. My grandpa's father heaved a sigh and said, 'The smell is very suspicious.'

My grandpa's father used to notice everything, and kept saying, 'These are not good signs. The smell is very suspicious.' He told my grandma, 'My daughter, what are these things happening around here? People appear out of nowhere, and then vanish into nothing. In the middle of last night, I woke up and felt like having a puff. I barely sat up and said to myself that it would be nice to have a smoke, when someone said, "Yes sir, I will prepare it for you." And then, to my surprise, a person lighted some tobacco and placed it in my hookah. Who are these people?'

What could my grandmother say? She just

remained silent. My grandfather also decided not to say anything, though he had understood by then what was going on. But my grandpa's father would sniff the air around him, and say, 'This is not good. The smell is very suspicious.'

My mother used to go out often for a walk with her grandfather. People they met on the street would want to show their respect to my grandpa's father by touching his feet or greeting him with folded hands, and ask him how he was doing. But my grandpa's father would say, 'Wait a minute! First let me touch you and smell you, and only then we can talk.' So saying, he would tap these persons with his hand, smell them, and talk to them only if he was satisfied. Of course he could not be blamed. At that time, among the people who were seen on the streets of Domohani, seventy five percent were not real people. No one bothered about it, because everyone was used to it.

It is very strange how people get used to something. I can talk about my mother's eldest brother. He developed a tremendous fear of ghosts long before they moved to Domohani. Again, he could not be blamed. Who isn't afraid of ghosts at that age? But he was a bit more scared than others. Whenever he had to go out of his room after dark, he needed a companion. This habit stayed with him even after they had moved to Domohani. One evening, he was studying with his tutor Dharmadas babu. They were alone in the house, the others had gone out for a walk. At that time, he felt like going to the bathroom. He could not possibly tell his teacher to come along with him. So, seeing no alternative, he went into the house, and addressed the darkness there, 'Can anyone hear me?'

No sooner had he uttered these words, a boy of roughly his age came and said, 'You want to say something?'

'I will have to go to the bathroom, can you come with me and stand guard there?'

The boy burst into laughter. He said, 'Why do you need that? What are you afraid of?'

My uncle snapped, 'Don't try to be funny. You will stand there because I have asked you to stand there.'

The boy stood outside the bathroom anyway. When my uncle came out of the bathroom, he said, 'But you haven't yet told me what it is that you are afraid of.'

My uncle said very seriously, 'Ghosts.'

The boy started laughing and vanished into thin air. My uncle got quite angry, and muttered to himself, 'You guys have really become over-smart.'

So this was how things were in Domohani. Nobody cared. Only my grandpa's father sniffed the air, sniffed everyone around himself. One day he was coming back from the marketplace. He had a small basket in his hand in which he was carrying some catfish. On the way, one fish climbed out of the basket, made it to the road and started to run away. My grandpa's father was trying desperately to put that fish back into the basket, afraid that the fish would sting if he did not hold it properly. At this time, someone appeared there, and very cordially, caught the fish with his hand, put it into the basket, and started to go on his way. My grandpa's father stopped him, sniffed him, and said, 'This is not good. The smell is very suspicious. Who are you? Tell me, who are you in particular, and who are all of you in general?'

My grandpa's father blocked his way. The person did not lose his nerve at all. Suddenly he bent forward a little, sniffed my grandpa's father, and told him, 'This is not good. The smell is very suspicious. Who are you? Tell me.'

And so saying, he vanished into thin air.

From then on, my grandpa's father never talked about the smell. He looked somewhat serious. The insult that came from the ghost really hurt his prestige. Can you imagine, a ghost smelled him and said all those words! Unthinkable.

Translated by Palash Baran Pal

The Many Faces of
Barada Charan

Detective Barada Charan was a very clever man no doubt, but his behaviour was somewhat weird. He never did what ordinary people did. When entering someone's house, he rarely used the front gate. He preferred to enter by climbing the boundary wall at the back of the house, or by scaling the rainwater pipes to the roof, or in some such strange way. If he wanted to go to Mogra, he would get on a mail train. He knew fully well that mail trains do not stop at Mogra. And yet that was what he would do, and jump out of the moving train at Mogra. In blazing sunshine, he was seen wearing a raincoat and a pair of high boots. It was not easy to understand why he sometimes wore overcoats in summer. He was a master at donning disguises. And because he was in disguise all the time, people forgot what he actually looked like. Sometimes he had twirled whiskers, sometimes a flowing moustache, sometimes a French-style goatee, sometimes a long beard like Rabindranath, sometimes wavy hair, sometimes needle-like hair, sometimes he wore red sunglasses, sometimes black sunglasses, sometimes blue sunglasses. Sometimes with blackened teeth he looked like a toothless old man wandering around with a stick in hand, sometimes in a turban he appeared to be a Sikh. Because of many such disguises, even his family members had begun to forget what he actually looked like.

The other day, Barada Charan's mother called a woman hawker to buy some dried cow-dung to be used as fuel. At that time, she noticed a mole on the left side of the hawker's nose and suspected that the person was, in fact, Barada. The point was that at that time Barada Charan had gone away for a few days to conduct an investigation, and there was no news of him. So she exclaimed,

'Goodness gracious, aren't you Barada?' But the cow-dung hawker was not Barada after all. However, the hawker had to face a lot of trouble because of this incident.

On another occasion, Barada Charan's father saw a man with a sooty face emerging from Barada's room. He caught hold of him and started shouting, 'Thief! Thief!' People from the neighborhood gathered around, the thief was detained, but the thief kept on claiming that he was Barada. Even when his false hair and beard was pulled off and the soot on his face was washed, Barada Charan's father kept insisting that the person could not possibly be Barada, because Barada looked very different. Barada's mother said repeatedly, 'This is my son Barada,' but no one believed her. After all, she was the one who mistook the cow-dung hawker for Barada a few days ago. From time to time, such confusion would often arise involving Barada.

Ram babu's daughter was going to get married. Ram babu was rich. He bought about two hundred thousand rupees' worth of gold jewellery. He was feeling uneasy with so much jewellery at home. So he went looking for Barada Charan.

At that time, Barada Charan was in the disguise of a hermit with long hair and a long beard, observing with a magnifying glass, with undivided attention, something that looked like a small stick.

Ram babu said, 'Barada, you will have to keep a watch on my daughter's jewellery. The wedding is just two days away, I am worried.'

Barada Charan smiled and said, 'Alright, I will be there.'

Within an hour of Ram babu's returning home, Barada Charan appeared in his hermit's disguise. In a low voice, he asked Ram babu, 'Where have you kept all the gold?'

'In the safe in the corner room. Come on, I will show you.'

Once in the corner room, Barada Charan looked around the room. He then asked for the safe's key, and examined it thoroughly. He opened the safe and looked at the jewellery as well. Finally, he said, 'Don't worry. Relax and do whatever you have to do now.'

Ram babu felt assured by Barada's words and went to do something else. About an hour later, a Kabuliwallah arrived. Ram babu was surprised, and asked him, 'What do you want?'

The Kabuliwallah said, in a hushed tone, 'I am Barada, I have come to keep watch on the jewellery.'

What was that supposed to mean? Ram babu was completely dumbfounded. He stuttered and said, 'But Barada is already here, watching the jewellery!'

The Kabuliwallah's eyes widened, 'Disaster! Let's go quickly and find out what's going on there.'

In the corner room, they found that the safe door was ajar, and there was no trace of the jewellery. And the hermit had vanished.

Ram babu covered his face with his hands and sat down. The Kabuliwallah gnashed his teeth in anger.

The next incident happened at Gadadhar babu's home. He was also a very rich man. He had a hobby of collecting rare and valuable gems from around the world. He had built a strong room in his house, where he kept all these gems. He had three or four very loyal security guards. Once he got a letter from an unknown source, which said, 'This Wednesday night, at 11 pm, bring the egg-sized Burmese pearl that you have and leave it on the altar beneath the banyan tree on the south side of the crematorium. If you fail to do so, you will be murdered within seven days.'

Gadadhar babu sent for Barada Charan immediately. Barada Charan came in the disguise of a fakir, listened to the story solemnly, and said, 'Alright, you should go to the crematorium on the scheduled day. I will accompany you.'

On Wednesday, Barada Charan reached Gadadhar's house by 7 pm. He said, 'Let's go. It's better to go a little early. The sky is overcast, it may rain. You will leave the pearl there, and then I will take over.'

That was what was done. Gadadhar went with Barada Charan in fakir's attire, left the pearl in the place mentioned in the letter, and came back home. Around nine o'clock, the fakir appeared again in his house.

Gadadhar babu exclaimed, 'What happenned, Barada? Why did you come back?'

'What do you mean by "come back"? Let's go, we will have to go to the crematorium.'

'But I just went there with you and came back a little while ago!'

The fakir was taken aback, and said, 'Disaster! What did you do there? Have you left the pearl there?'

'That's what you asked me to do!'

The fakir shook his head violently and said, 'Not I, Gadadhar babu, I swear to God.'

But Gadadhar babu did not pay heed to him. He filed a complaint with the police, accusing Barada Charan of stealing the pearl by tricking him.

The police went to Barada Charan's house to

arrest him and found that a person was painting the walls of the house. The police officer knew about Barada Charan's knack for disguises. So he arrested the painter without any hesitation and declared, 'There's a theft case against you, Barada babu.'

The painter almost burst into tears and said, 'But I am not Barada babu, sir.'

'Why are you putting on an act? I know you well enough.'

The painter pleaded and cried, but the police officer was not to be swayed. The man was taken to the police station. Finally, when his wife, children and neighbours came and certified that he was not Barada, the officer let him go.

But Barada had to be arrested. So the officer hid in Barada's room with two constables. When Barada Charan's old aunt came into the room in the evening with incense sticks, he caught her by the neck and said, 'Now I got you, Barada, now you cannot get away.'

Barada's aunt screamed at the top of her voice.

People from nearby houses came running. It was a big scandal. The officer was humiliated and he went back to the police station. However, he kept getting news off and on about someone seeing Barada Charan at some place or other. One person reported that Barada Charan was standing in the western meadow in the disguise of a palm tree. Another person said that Barada Charan had become a cow and hidden himself in the cow-shed of the Samantas. Eight beggars, two Kabuliwallahs, three Sikhs, three sadhus, two fakirs, five old women and six old men were picked up one by one and questioned for hours at the police station with the suspicion that they were, in fact, Barada.

Needless to say, Barada Charan was nowhere to be found.

The police office said in desperation, 'I am thinking and thinking, and see no end to the problem. I will not be able to eat or sleep well until I find Barada Charan. By the way, I hope your pearl was insured.'

Gadadhar babu heaved a sigh and said, 'Yes it was. But money is not everything. It was such a rare piece!'

The police officer fumed at his own inefficiency.

Ram babu came to the police and said that he strongly suspected that his daughter's jewellery had also been stolen by Barada Charan.

But Barada Charan could not be found. The cases of the pearl and the jewellery remained unsolved.

Once, in the dead of night, Gadadhar babu was asleep in the first floor room in his house. Suddenly, he woke up at some faint sound. First he suspected a rat in the room. Then it seemed to him that the sound was coming from the window.

Gadadhar babu got up with a flashlight in hand. He could not see anyone at the window. But he saw an envelope lying on the floor. He opened it and read the letter inside. It said, 'We want to return your pearl to you. You will have to pay only five hundred thousand rupees as our fees. The pearl is with us, don't worry about it.'

Gadadhar babu was deeply perturbed after reading the letter. He dressed quickly, called his servants who woke up the chauffeur. The car was brought out of the garage and Gadadhar babu set out on a journey in the middle of the night.

The car stopped in front of a house in a small town about ten miles away. The house belonged to a widowed sister of Gadadhar babu.

He hollered from outside. A young man, obviously awakened by the voice, opened the door and said, 'Uncle! What are you doing here at this hour? Is something the matter?' Gadadhar babu held the letter in front of him and said, 'What does this mean?'

The guy was surprised. He started scratching his head and said, 'But the pearl is . . .'

Gadadhar babu chided in a low voice, 'Yes the pearl is with you. So who wrote the letter?'

'I think somebody is trying to play a game.'

Gadadhar babu said, 'Whatever it might be, I want to see the pearl with my own eyes.'

'Come in, I'll show you.'

Gadadhar babu entered the house with his nephew, climbed the stairs to the attic. There, his nephew pulled on a piece of string. Tied to the end which was hanging inside the rainwater pipe, was a paper packet. The packet was opened and it was found that the pearl was where it should have been.

Gadadhar babu heaved a sigh of relief and said, 'What a relief! I was worried to death. Now, once I get the payment from the insurance company, I will sell the pearl to Thakkarlal. All negotiations have been finalised.'

They hung the pearl at the end of the string again and saw that the driver was standing at the door.

Gadadhar babu was very displeased. He said, 'What's this? Why are you here? Did we call you?'

'No, no one called me. I had to come up on my own initiative. No no no no, don't take your pistol out. I have a pistol in my hand.'

Gadadhar babu felt his hands becoming limp. He asked, 'Who are you?'

'Take a guess.'

A wave of suspicion was churning in Gadadhar babu. He said, 'Could you be Barada?'

'You are right, this is Barada Charan, always at your service. You had made an excellent plan. Ram babu had bought a big diamond along with all the other jewellery for his daughter's wedding. You dressed your nephew as a hermit and pocketed that diamond. After that, you devised another plan to steal your own pearl. Your nephew arrived at your house two hours before me in the guise of a fakir. Everyone in your house, including the servants and the guards, could bear witness to the fact that I came in a fakir's dress, which is exactly what you wanted. But you cannot have the last laugh. No no, I will knock your head off. Can't you hear the sound of the heavy boots on the stairs? That's the police force.'

That was the police force indeed. With the officer leading the way.

Translated by Palash Baran Pal

Detective
Barada Charan

Detective Barada Charan was engrossed in thought regarding the case of a stolen gourd. Somebody (or bodies) had stolen a plump gourd from the rooftop of Grandma Mokkhoda of Naparha. Grandma Mokkhoda's grandson worked far away from home, and he loved gourds cooked in lentils. So grandma had saved the gourd for her grandson, who was supposed to arrive in a day or two. Meanwhile, day before yesterday, the gourd was stolen. Grandma came crying to Barada Charan, 'Dear little Barada, bring my gourd back to me.'

And since then, Barada Charan had lost his sleep and appetite. All day, he had been searching around with a magnifying glass in hand, accompanied by his assistant and his dog. He was looking for clues in Grandma Mokkhoda's hut, its roof, and even in the dwellings of her neighbours. And then, on coming back home, he analysed his findings throughout the day, made notes with a pen, and sometimes muttered to himself, pronouncing things like 'Hmm!', or 'No, that's not it' or something similar.

Barada Charan was about thirty years old. He had his old mother at home, and his assistant-cum-nephew Chakku, and a pet dog called Donkey. Barada Charan was a well-built man, and kept his body fit with adequate exercises. His nephew Chakku was thin, but he knew Judo. Donkey was an expert in barking.

Chakku kept asking again and again, 'Have you reached any conclusion, uncle?'

Barada said absent-mindedly, 'Looking at the stalk, it seems that the gourd was quite big.'

'That's right, it was.'

'The gourd was not cut from its stalk. It was twisted and wrenched.'

'Yes, you are right.'

'A big gourd was twisted and wrenched from its stalk on a tin roof, and yet there was no sound. Too many mosquitos sneaked into Grandma Mokkhoda's mosquito-net, so she could not sleep well. If there was any sound on the roof, she ought to have heard it.'

Chakku seemed thoughtful when he replied, 'That's true, but don't forget that Grandma Mokkhoda is a little short of hearing.'

At this point Donkey started barking outside, and someone shouted, 'Mind your dog.'

Chakku ran out. A little later, an impressive-looking man entered the room and said, 'Barada babu, I have a murder case for you.'

Barada Charan gravely asked him to sit down, pulled out his case diary notebook, got ready with a pen, and said, 'Give me the details.'

'My pet cockatoo was found hanging from its perch this morning, dead.'

Barada Charan squinted and said, 'And you think that this is an unnatural death?'

'Naturally,' said the man, somewhat distraught.

'My neighbour Ramchandra had his eyes on the bird for a long time. He often told me, "Ambujakkho, your cockatoo sings God Hari's name so sweetly!" I always suspected his intentions. This morning, when I saw the bird hanging, I examined the water and the food that was given to it. I think either the water or the food was poisoned.'

Barada Charan closed his notebook and got up, took his pistol from the drawer and put it in his pocket. He took a magnifying glass, some rope, a camera, and also, for some reason, the tape-recorder. He asked Chakku and Donkey to get ready as well. Then he looked at the gentleman and said, 'Ambujakkho babu, the case may not be that simple. Of course Ramchandra babu might have had some motive. But then the cockatoo might have committed suicide. Or maybe there is some deeper conspiracy behind all this.'

While Barada was on his way out, his mother called him and said, 'Why don't you eat some wet rice before you go out?'

But Barada Charan did not pay heed to her. He went out.

Ambujakkho babu's house was fairly big. There was a covered verandah at the back of the house, containing a huge number of cages, with a lot of birds chirping in them.

Barada Charan examined the cockatoo's cage very carefully. The bird was still hanging from the perch, with a chain tied to its legs. At the ends of the perch, he saw two bowls, containing water and chick peas. Barada Charan picked up one bean of chick pea and threw it towards the courtyard behind the house. A crow swooped down immediately and ate it. Barada Charan stared at the crow for a while. It didn't die. That meant the chick peas were not poisoned. Barada Charan sucked some water into a dropper. He looked around and found Ambujakkho's pet Kabuli cat sitting on a wooden box. With a sudden move, Barada Charan grabbed it. Before Ambujakkho could lodge any protest, he made the cat open its mouth through a strange trick, and poured the water from the dropper into the oral cavity of the cat. The cat said something in protest, but it did not die.

Barada Charan solemnly pronounced, 'Hmm.'

Meanwhile, Ambujakkho took a few globules of homeopathic medicine and muttered, 'I'm aching all over.'

Chakku was wandering around the house with Donkey on a leash, looking for clues. He came running back and whispered into Barada Charan's ears, 'Rind of gourds. Lots of them, scattered behind Ramchandra Babu's house!'

Barada Charan moved with lightning speed.

Ramchandra, an old man, was reading the Ramayan in his room. He was visibly surprised when he saw Barada Charan, and said, 'Hello Barada babu. Come in, come in. It's an honour to get to see famous people like you.'

Barada Charan sat down and studied Ramchandra babu for a while with an ice-cold stare.

Ramchandra babu closed his Ramayan and said, 'I was thinking of going to see you today.

Last night, somebody (or bodies) stole six coconuts from the tree in my garden. Very mysterious! It is difficult for anyone to enter my garden from outside. But of course . . .'

At this point, Ramchandra babu paused very suggestively.

Barada Charan started writing the case in his diary and said, 'Don't conceal any information, Ramchandra babu.'

Ramchandra babu smiled shyly and said, 'I know, there is no point concealing anything. I cannot possibly fool you. So it's best that I let it out.' Then he lowered his voice and said, 'Ambuj, who lives next door, is a big consumer of coconuts. He eats coconut meat all the time. He eats it fried in oil, or simmered in sugar syrup, or raw with puffed rice. I have never come across anyone who relishes coconuts as much as he does. Quite often he comes to me and says, "Ramchandra babu, your coconut trees are teeming with fruits." I suspect, last night . . .'

'Hmm.' Barada Charan assumed a very grave

look. A little while ago, he had seen Ambujakkho babu taking homeopathic globules for bodyache. No wonder he had bodyache! At his age, if someone climbed such tall coconut trees, quite naturally he would suffer from bodyache.

But, even after a long search, no coconut or even coconut rind was found in Ambujakkho's house. This was mysterious as well. Because if you knew someone who was a coconut-addict, it would be unnatural not to find any trace of a coconut in his house.

Gourd-skin, on the other hand, was found behind Ramchandra babu's house, as Chakku described. Very clear clue.

But Barada Charan never did anything in a hurry. He gave ample time to the culprits. The culprit could not even guess that he was being suspected.

Right around noon time, Barada Charan went to Grandma Mokkhoda's house to ask her a few additional questions. The questions were like these: what was the colour of the gourd, dark green or pale green? Were there any wormholes on the surface of the gourd? In fact, there was even some evidence of nail marks near the stem. Barada Charan found all these unmistakable signs among all the gourd-skin that he could find in the dumpster behind Ramchandra babu's house.

While he was interrogating Grandma Mokkhoda, Chakku suddenly appeared and whispered in Barada Charan's ear, 'Uncle, there is a huge bag of coconut rind in Grandma Mokkhoda's store room. Plus six coconuts, rinds shaven.'

Barada Charan's head spun. The different cases were becoming intertwined and therefore complicated. Grandma Mokkhoda did not have any coconut tree in her house, so how come there were coconuts or coconut-rind in her house? On the other hand, the coconuts stolen from Ramchandra babu's garden could not be found in Ambujakkho's house. And, surprise surprise! The number found in Grandma Mokkhoda's house tallied with the number stolen.

Barada Charan left with these thoughts. He took the pistol out of his pocket and checked whether all six chambers were loaded. They were indeed.

As soon as he landed on the street, a car screeched to a stop by him. Inside, there was a respectable-looking man. He joined his palms and said, 'Please get in. Let me have the pleasure of giving a ride to the famous detective.'

Barada Charan got in. Chakku and Donkey occupied the front seat. The unknown man lowered his voice and said, 'A very mysterious thing has happened. My old pet cockatoo died yesterday. It was my favourite. I decided that I would bury the bird in some good place and build a fantastic mausoleum for it. But there was a problem. I put the dead body of the bird in a nylon bag, left it on the front porch and went to look for my driver, whom I wanted to ask to take the car out of the garage. When I came back, the bag was gone. Can you imagine that, what a monstrous incident! I implore you to take the case.'

Barada Charan noted down everything in his diary. He pronounced gravely, 'Hmm. So I now have two cockatoo cases. That's strange!'

A perplexed Barada Charan got down as the car reached his home.

Barada Charan was very absent-minded when he started taking his lunch. He was not even aware of what he was eating. Gourd, cockatoos, coconut: everything created a maze in his head. His mother requested, 'Why don't you take a little more rice and have it with the gourd curry?'

The phrase 'gourd curry' rang a few bells in Barada Charan's head. Frankly, there was nothing to be surprised about, because gourd curry was a frequent lunch dish for him.

And then, suddenly he straightened up and said, 'Gourd curry? Where did the gourd come from? I didn't buy any gourd at the marketplace today!'

His mother said, 'Did I ever say that you bought it? Of course you didn't. Chakku brought it. One of his friends has grown a lot of gourds. Apparently he has given one to Chakku.'

Barada Charan looked at his own plate intently. By the side of the gourd curry, there lay two fried nuggets. He got up and fetched his magnifying glass and started looking at them with great attention. His mother said, 'What are you looking at? These are coconut fries. Chakku brought six coconuts. He said they fell from a tree because of a mighty wind. I have taken the meat out of the kernel of two of them and made these nuggets.'

During the rest of the lunch, Barada Charan did not really eat much. Finally he got up. Chakku had finished his lunch long ago and gone to some teacher's house for some help with his studies.

Barada Charan took his pistol and magnifying glass. Holding Donkey's leash in his hands, he went out of his house. He started looking all around. After some time, Donkey understood his intentions and led him to the cattle-shed. There, he saw a recently-bought cage, and a cockatoo, very much alive, sitting on the perch. On seeing Barada Charan, it started reciting, 'Lord Hari Lord Hari Lord Hari, we sing to his endless glory.'

Barada Charan brought his tape-recorder and started recording the bird's words.

Then, throughout the afternoon, Barada Charan was immersed in a pool of thoughts involving gourd, cockatoo and coconut, much like Archimedes pondering about specific gravity in the bathtub. At the end, he leaped up, very much like Archimedes had done when he said 'Eureka'. The entire mystery became crystal clear to him.

To be sure, he now realised that the person who stole the gourd from Grandma Mokkhoda's house was the same as the person who played a magician's trick on the dead cockatoo belonging to the person who gave a ride. He was also the same person who put it in the cage in Ambujakkho babu's house, and vanished with the cockatoo which sang Lord Hari's name. And for some unknown reason, picked six coconuts from Ramayan-lover Ramchandra babu's garden. And he was the same culprit, who in an effort to erase the evidence as well as to confuse the investigation, brought the news of gourd skin lying behind Ramchandra babu's house, and revealed the existence of coconut rind at Grandma Mokkhoda's house.

It was late in the night. Everyone was fast asleep. Barada Charan almost silently went to the next room with a pistol in his hand and stared at the darkness. He could make out, Chakku was sleeping by his grandma's side.

Detective Barada Charan heaved a sigh. He would not do anything at the moment. He always gave more opportunities to the culprits. That way, the culprit had no idea he was being observed. And then one day he would weave the net around himself.

Barada Charan lowered his pistol and came back to his room. Now he was sure who the culprit was. It was no other than . . .

Translated by Palash Baran Pal

So Then

Detective Baradacharan got down from the top of the cupboard, leaning on the shoulders of his nephew Konchi, with a lot of grime and dust all over him and a lizard perched on his shoulder, and said in a serious tone, 'Hmm!' Hearing that hmm, the impoverished landlord Bajrakundal saw some light of hope and asked eagerly, 'Got any clue, son?' Baradacharan was a man of few words. He crawled under a huge bed, shone his flashlight through a maze of pots and pitchers and boxes, and said again in a sombre voice, 'Hmm!'

Bajrakundal did not really hope that he would find the valuable gold watch that dated back from his grandfather's time. He had summoned Detective Baradacharan, who lived close to his home, just for some mental satisfaction. He heaved a sigh and said, 'Very little is left of our property. Now we are losing the few valuable things that are left. Well, if you can find this one, I will praise your luck.'

No sound was heard from Baradacharan, who was still under the bed. Baradacharan never lost his concentration while working. His clients might not have much confidence in his ability, but they were bound to have a lot of respect for his methods and his practices. He was not an ordinary man in any way. For example, he never entered his own house or anyone else's house through the front door. Detectives are not supposed to. So he had to climb the boundary walls, or force his way through the hedges, or scale the water pipes to the roof. He also had some unique methods of investigation. If he heard that the thief had entered through the northern side of the house, he would begin his investigation on the southern side.

Anyway, it had been two days since he was conducting an investigation in the old, huge and dilapidated house of Bajrakundal. So far, he had climbed to the top of at least fifty cupboards, crawled under twenty beds, and had finished searching almost all of the twenty-five rooms of the house. And yet he could not find the watch. After about half an hour, he resurfaced with more dust and grime all over his body and a baby mouse in his pocket, and said, 'Hmm!' Bajrakundal had heard that 'hmm' at least a hundred times since the previous day, and each time he saw some ray of hope in it. This time as well, he asked, 'Any clue?'

Baradacharan said in an irritated tone, 'What do you want: clue, or watch? There are many clues. But I thought you wanted the watch.' Bajrakundal said with a sad face, 'Of course I want the watch, son. You know my financial condition. The jeweller Nimé wanted to buy the watch for two hundred rupees. I thought of using the money to have a quilt made for the winter.' Baradacharan said, 'Hmm.' And then, without wasting any more words, he opened a huge wooden chest and rummaged through the loads of torn and damaged quilts that were inside it. Konchi advised Bajrakundal in a whispering tone, 'Why don't you have your bath, eat your lunch and take a little afternoon nap? When my uncle is looking for it, it will surely be discovered if it exists somewhere in this world.' Bajrakundal replied, 'It is in this world, my child, it hasn't gone very far. My grandson Hemkundal, a true menace, tied it to the neck of our pet cat Dugga. Dugga has not left the house. So the watch must be lying somewhere around.' At this point, Baradacharan suddenly raised his eyes from the wooden chest and asked, 'Can you give me a loincloth, about four cubits long?'

'Loincloth?' Bajrakundal was surprised, 'What are you going to do with that?' Barada glared at his face and said, 'I will tie it around my neck and try to commit suicide.' Bajrakundal fetched a big loincloth and said, 'Okay, give it to me when you are done. I will also do the same.' Baradacharan glared at him one more time, took off his clothes and tied the loincloth tightly around his waist. Then he went straight to the old pond in the inner portion of the house. It was a very deep pond. The steps leading to the water were made of good stone. Some of the stones had weathered with time, but the grandeur of the flight of stairs was still unmistakable. Baradacharan paid no attention to Konchi or to Bajrakundal, and plunged into the pond. He filled his lungs with air, and then plunged again into the depths of the faint green water. In the first dip, he could not fathom the water. After about a minute, he surfaced, took a deep breath, and dipped again. And then once again. And once more. He did not leave out any side of the pond: east, west, north, south, north-west, north-east, south-west, south-east. Finally, after about two hours, he demanded breathlessly, 'A crowbar.'

Bajrakundal ran and fetched a big crowbar, and asked, 'Got any clue, son?' Baradacharan did not reply. He took the crowbar in his hand, and dived near the western end of the pond. As he went down into the water, his feet eventually touched a place where two large slabs of stone were placed side by side. Barada put the crowbar between the two pieces and gave it a push. The stones parted. Baradacharan rose up, took a deep breath, plunged again and this time gave a tweak to the rusted iron door that lay behind the stone slabs. The door opened. Baradacharan took a new installment of air, and started swimming below the surface of water to enter through the door, swam through a submerged tunnel in a somewhat upward direction where he could breath again, and rest his feet on a surface. It was pitch dark. He kept advancing by feeling the way with the crowbar. He found a wooden door in front of him. Very thick wood. A big lock was hanging on the door. But how could the door and the lock stop Baradacharan if he had a crowbar with him? Within two minutes, Baradacharan entered the underground room. He started feeling around with his hands, and found that there were ten to twelve iron chests in the room. He murmured to himself, 'Hmm.' Then he came up above water, when others had given up on the possibility of his being alive. And he announced, 'Found.'

Bajrakundal eagerly questioned, 'What? Clue, or watch?' Baradacharan shook his head and said, 'No. Neither clue nor watch. I am not even thrilled by what I got. But anyway, scoop out all the water from the pond. And don't tell anybody anything.' 'But what should we get by emptying the pond?' Bajrakundal asked. Barada said, 'Not the watch,' and started putting on his clothes somberly. Lots of people gathered to empty the pond with the hope of getting some good fish in the process. Within two days, all water and all fish were gone. When evening fell, Baradacharan went down the flight of steps along with Bajrakundal and Konchi, with a lamp in his hand. They stood before the two slabs of stone covered with mud and moss. Cleverly, Baradacharan had pushed the two slabs next to each other. Otherwise, people would have discovered the tunnel while emptying the pond.

On reaching the underground room through the tunnel, Baradacharan said very nonchalantly, 'Those chests contain hidden treasure from your ancestors. Open them and see for yourself.' Bajrakundal almost fainted, but finally held his ground. With an axe and a crowbar, all twelve chests were opened one by one. Some contained gold coins, some contained diamonds and others gems, some contained silver money, and some contained gold and silver utensils. It was a veritable treasure trove! Bajrakundal was beside himself at the sight. He started weeping in delight, 'I have gone through very hard times since my childhood. In order to maintain the norms of our estate, I had trouble making both ends meet. Now at last God has smiled at me.' Baradacharan, sitting on the lid of a wooden chest and thinking deeply about something, said absent-mindedly, 'Hmm. But if the cat hadn't gone out of the house, then the watch must be . . .' Bajrakundal interrupted excitedly, 'Forget the watch. With whatever I have found here, I can buy thousands of such watches.'

Baradacharan glared at Bajrakundal. Then he sunk into his own thoughts again and murmured to himself, 'The last time the cat was seen by the side of the pond. Before that, it was spotted on the roof of the decaying music room. But the watch is in none of these places. So then . . .'

Bajrakundal held Baradacharan's hands and said, 'I will give you a million rupees. Do you understand? A million. Now forget about the watch.' Baradacharan freed his hands and kept murmuring, 'If the cat hadn't come near the pond, it must have gone to . . .', and, while saying so, he came out of the tunnel and started walking towards the eroding kitchen. Bajrakundal followed him and kept saying, 'I don't want the watch any more. I will happily give you a million rupees.' Baradacharan shook his head and said, 'No. My fee is one hundred rupees. And that, too, if I can find the watch.'

'But one can buy hundreds of thousands of watches with this wealth.' Baradacharan pouted his lips and said, 'The gold, the coins, the diamonds, all these things are irrelevant for this investigation.' He kept moving around, murmuring to himself, 'The cat and the watch are related. If the cat hasn't stepped outside the house, one would naturally believe that the watch also hasn't gone out of the house. So then . . .'

Translated by Palash Baran Pal